The Innswich Horror

EDWARD LEE

deadite
press

DEADITE PRESS
205 NE BRYANT
PORTLAND, OR 97217

AN ERASERHEAD PRESS COMPANY
WWW.ERASERHEADPRESS.COM

ISBN: 1-936383-11-X

"The Innswich Horror" first appeared as a limited edition hardback by Cemetery Dance, 2010.

Printed in the USA.

ACKNOWLEDGMENTS: Foremost, the author must thank the late, great H. P. Lovecraft for providing thirty years of horrific wonder and demented influence. I must also thank the late Brian McNaughton for early influences. Also Tim McGinnis, Bob Strauss, Richard Chizmar, and Ian Levy. I am further in debt to authors S. T. Joshi, Darrell Schweitzer, and Anthony Pearsall for their various preeminent books on the life and works of HPL. Please forgive any misrepresentations and/or errors.

For Wendy Brewer. Be my Cthulheena.

The motor-coach noise provided an aural mental backdrop: I imagined myself as the Master, and fancied I could see what *he* would see beyond the drab window. Not common fields, unremarkable treelines, and a typical New England summer sky but scenes much more sinister. Blasted heaths pocking malnourished meadows and dying scrubland, trees twisted and lightning-scarred, and a sky onerous and swollen with menace. And there–yes!–over the rusted iron railing-work of a decades-old bridge, my gaze was commandeered by the sluggish Miskatonic, in whose depths God knew what lurked or lay bloated in death or states *worse* than death. The prosaic bus window was no longer a simple transparent pane but a prism-obscura, a looking-glass to eldritch sights, nether-chasms, and leaky rives betwixt dimensions and inconteplatable horrors. Then I blinked–

–and slumped with a smile. It was just the rushing and very healthy Essex River below and, to either side, an endless rise of pine and oak. No, though God had possessed me with an ample grasp for learning, I was not so possessed by even an irreducible fraction of the Master's imagination. I suppose that's why I delighted so in his tales. Imagination, indeed, was a gift better reveled in by true scribes of the fantastical.

Scribes such as Howard Phillips Lovecraft.

I shared the bus with but a half-dozen other fellows, men of hard labor, judging by their appearance; and I dared wonder if Lovecraft himself had ever ridden this same bus. If so: *Which seat? Which window did he gaze past to titillate his muse?* It was a funny thing, such reverence to this manner of fiction. Just as HPL was obsessed with everything from the cosmos to colonial architecture, I, it seems, am obsessed with his work.

My name is Foster Morley, thirty-three years of age, brown-haired and brown-eyed. I suppose Lovecraft might describe me as nondescript and unobtrusive, but he would likely be amused by a certain parallel. Like so many of his protagonists, I come from solid English gentry and family means, wealthy by legacy, and hold an unutilized degree from Brown University. I occupy a 180-year-old manse in stately Providence, near the Athenaeum, where my family bloodline migrated to before the Revolution. That family is now deceased, I the only offspring. Hence, by the grace of my Creator, my days are dreams in which I want for nothing, and when I am not philanthrophising . . . I read. I read Lovecraft, over and over again, for never have mere words on paper been able to transport me to other, more interesting worlds. Worlds not akin to this one at all–with its financial depression and its unfathomable wars. No, but instead worlds of dreadful wonder and daedalic terror.

Oddly, I was never aware of Lovecraft until I read an obituary in the *Providence Evening Bulletin* over two years ago, in March of 1937, commenting on the local academic fantasist's passing and strange career. Curiosity piqued, then, I lucked upon the June, 1936, issue of the magazine *Weird Tales* and pored over "Shadow Out of Time." From that point, I was duly habituated, after which I expended minor sums but fastidious effort in making everything the Master wrote a constituent of my library. My obsession was at hand, and more than that–perhaps my salvation. Though content in my companionless solitude, I now had something bereft to me for so long: mental substance, a trip to lost terrascapes every night, rather than counting tedious hours of vacuity.

I took to re-reading his work at the tree by his grave at Swan Point Cemetery; I strolled weekly past his rooming-house in College Street and would always stop to peer out upon Federal Hill and spy St. John's Catholic Church, his model for his last tale in earnest, the brilliant "Haunter of the Dark"; I'd prowl Angell Street and Benefit, hoping that some psychic lingering of the icon might brush by me– or somehow bestow a macabre, ethereal blessing; I'd even shop weekly at the Weybosset's Store where he so often spent his pittance on food. More than once, too, I railed to New York, to stare up in awe at the squalid Flatbush rowhouse where the Master lived off and on with his wife; most recently I lit a votive at St. Paul's Chapel on Broadway, where they married. I took to traveling where *he* traveled: from Marblehead to the District of Columbia to New Orleans, from Wilbraham, Massachusetts, to Dunedin, Florida–and exclusively by steam-train or motor coach, for this afforded me to see what he saw on the same long and clattering jaunts. That process–*seeing*–was most crucial to me, seeing and being where he had been. I once stood at the foot of Poe's grave in Baltimore, only because I knew that Lovecraft had stood there once as well. I even tried to purchase the looming gable-manse at 135 Benefit Street but the owners would not sell, even for the preposterous price I offered, this being, of course, the nefarious, lichen-enslimed "shunned" house.

Obsessed? Without doubt. An alienist, I'm certain, would label me with some syndrome close to clinical, something analytically Jungian. Through Lovecraft's words I know that I was desperately in search of something, and I'll only know what that something is when I find it.

Er, pardon me. I should say that I've already found it–in Innswich–perhaps to my eternal turmoil.

I'd left the servants in charge–they were quite used to my junkets of inexplicable travel by now–and had decided to retrace the fictive journey of one of his characters, that character being the unnamed protagonist of my very favorite tale, *The Shadow Over Innsmouth.* HPL's own notes, according to his confidant August Derleth, name the hapless fictional character as *Robert Olmstead,* though the name never appears in the actual story. It is not difficult to see, however, Mr. Olmstead's mirror-image to Lovecraft himself: an antiquary and architectural aficionado, traveling the depths of New England always by the least costly mode possible, to pursue his own obsessions.

This, then, would serve as my summer outing. Robert Olmstead departed Newburysport for Arkham on July 15, 1927, with the intention of perusing the witch-haunted town's archives and Colonial structure. Hence, my own desire to duplicate Olmstead's trip, again, to *see* what Lovecraft saw. Therefore, ever the stickler for detail, I commenced with my own sojourn on July, 15, 1939, leaving Newburysport from the same bus stop in front of the very real Hammond's Drug Store for the town of Salem, which was HPL's blueprint for Arkham.

I'd selected the forward-most seat on the coach, on the right-hand side, which afforded a spacious view through the windscreen. Several miles past the Essex now, the scenery seemed to denigrate in a manner that eludes sensible description; suddenly, the woods looked *impoverished*, the vegetation lost its summer luster, and even the road, paved only by crushed oyster shells, elicited the word *sallow*, though I know this sounds preposterously non-schematic. It was something, however, that existed beyond that month's record-breaking drought. An unchecked darkness settled in my spirit for reasons I cannot define.

Finally, through the windscreen, I took refreshing note of some sign of humanity: a rundown wood-slat shack–obviously a domicile--next to what appeared to be a smokehouse. A hog-pen, too, caught my eye, bounded by crude chicken wire and surrounding less than half a dozen swine. Something smelled appetizing, though, which I thought could only be from the smokehouse. Lastly a sign and roadside vending stand came into view. The sign read: ONDERDONK & SON. SMOKEHOUSE – FISH-FED PORK. At the same instant we passed, the driver seemed to grunt.

"Fish-fed pork?" I queried the driver. "I've never heard of that. Have you ever happened to try it?"

The driver's face remained forward, and at first I thought he had no intention of answering. "T'ain't nothin' I've ever et nor ever will. Same five hogs in that pen damn near year-long. More like fish-fed *skunk*, knowin' the Onderdonks. He and his kid–they'se furren. Don't like 'em, an' they'se don't like us."

A second of cogitation translated *furren* as foreign. I couldn't resist: "Us as in whom?"

"Don't matter!" the driver snapped. "Me, I'm just doin' my job. But them Onderdonks don't dare try to sell past the loop."

By now I had no conceivable idea what founded the driver's displeasure. "The loop?" I said more to myself.

"They sell that slop you call barbeque to migrants and plain folk who happen to be travelin' from New'bry to Salem, but they never take the loop in to town."

The perplexion steeped. I thought I'd best keep my queries to myself yet I also knew that the map showed no other town between Newburyport and Salem. "The town? You must mean Salem, but surely we're still an hour off at the least."

"No," he grumbled. Only now did I take notice of the driver's features–first recounting Lovecraft's story and the motor-man named Joe Sargent, cursed by that "Innsmouth look": narrow-headed, flat-nosed, crease-necked, with unblinking, over-protuberant eyes. Sargent's appearance causes in the mind of Robert Olmstead a spontaneous aversion. This fellow here, however, though surly in demeanor, was just a commonplace workingman.

"Olmstead," he said, "and here's the loop now." He veered aside and took a fork in the road, past a sign that read OLMSTEAD - 2 MILES - POP. 361. "This the only bus that goes there'n it's a fifteen-minute time-point."

It wasn't the fact that we were suddenly embarking toward a town I'd not heard of (not to mention a town not displayed on the map) but something else altogether. "*Olmstead?*" I pressed the word. "You're telling me there's an uncharted town called *Olmstead?*"

The question perturbed him. "It's on the time-table. We had a devil of a time tryin' to get the county to let us put in a bus stop; they made us *incorporate,* whatever that means 'sides havin' to pay a fee. Had to do the same to get mail delivery. T'ain't right that Olmsteaders shouldn't have no way to get to the bigger towns, especially the economy bein' the way it is," and then an abrupt thumb jerked over his shoulder to gesture the six other passengers sharing the coach with me. "Weren't for the fishin'," he added, "we'd be sunk."

Though these men must've heard the driver, their faces remained blank. They were unkempt, shabbily attired–fishermen, I saw, for they each had an armful of new fishing rods, plus several rolls of nets. It was clear they'd traveled to Newburyport to purchase these supplies. Still, though, the distraction of these rough but normal men didn't suffice to sway my major focus . . .

This is something. An arcane notion told me that mere coincidence wouldn't suffice to explain this. A town–Olmstead–sharing the name of Lovecraft's very protagonist in *The Shadow Over Innsmouth* . . .

The road narrowed, and grew more runneled, as my olfactory senses told me we were nearing the water. Suddenly an excitement usurped all other thoughts. Though Lovecraft traveled extensively his entire adult life, none of his travel logs that I knew of mentioned a town called Olmstead. *Had this town given Lovecraft the name of his main character?* I so hoped. *And if so, what would the town be like?*

The answer would be soon at hand.

2

It was an assailing disappointment that first swept me as the smoke-belching coach stopped in what I presumed was Olmstead's town-center. In fantasy, I thought I'd made a unique discovery: that I'd stumbled upon the true model for the Master's most masterful tale, and that at any moment now, I'd be envisioning Innsmouth's evilly-shadowed alleys, crumbling wharfs, and oddly angled, steep-roofed buildings rife with decrepitude and that "wormy decay" so ably conveyed by the tale's creator.

Instead I was greeted by nothing of the sort. Olmstead clearly owed its architecture to the utilitarian government block-house designs that came with the subsidized renewal projects of the late-'20s to early-'30s. What a let-down! Olmstead, indeed, was generic, not singular.

The bus seemed to hiccough smoke a full minute before the motor shut down. The half-dozen shabby fishermen stood from their seats simultaneously, then filed out, carrying their rods, tackle, and nets. "Fifteen minutes, in case ya want a breather and a stretch," informed the driver without looking at me. "You're goin' on to Salem, right?"

"Yes, sir. Thank you," I said and followed him off. He headed across the sterile street, toward a shop.

The smell of fish and low-tide gushed down the street from the direction I knew must be shoreward. Nothing at all like the aghast *reek* that so nauseated Robert Olmstead in the tale. The town-center left nothing particularized to describe, just block building after block building. Some must be apartments, for out from their windows hung laundry to dry; others must be businesses, though I detected not much in the way of local commerce. Now I had to smile at my overzealousness. The coincidence of the hidden town's name was clearly just that. *And this place, I thought, was no more a creative influence to Lovecraft than it would be an influence to any traveler: lackluster, unfeatured, insipid.*

When rising footsteps signaled me from this juvenile plunge of disappointment, I expected to find the chilly driver returning but instead looked up into the smiling face of a spry, good-conditioned man about my own age, or perhaps slightly younger, sharply dressed in conservative suit and tie, with dark-brown hair neatly combed. He carried a briefcase, and wore one of the smart beige Koko-Kooler hats, which were all the fashion rage among younger men these days. His expression seemed, oddly, one of relief, though I was certain we'd never before met.

"How do you do?" he greeted.

"I'm quite good, and hope you are as well."

"Sorry to intrude, but its just that your face seems a bit more welcome than the other men I've met here." His eyes glimpsed the cumbersome coach. "I take it you're traveling?"

"Why, yes. I'm going on to Salem. The name's Foster Morley—"

"William Garret," he returned and heartily shook my hand. Then he whispered, "Some odd ones in this town, eh?"

"None that I've yet noticed," I admitted. "Haven't seen anyone else about, other than you, I mean. You're obviously not an 'Olmsteader,' to use the driver's designation."

"No, I'm not. I'm from Boston, an accountant—er, I should say an *unemployed* accountant. So you haven't seen a blond fellow walking about, have you?"

"I'm sorry, no. I'm just taking a stretch before the coach is off again. Why do you ask?"

Now his deportment shifted to something more intense. "It's my friend, you see—his name's Poynter. We worked in the same accounting firm but both lost our jobs when this depression—as they're calling it—got the best of our business. He came here a month ago and recently wrote me. He found a job, I should say, but now I can't find *him*."

"Is that so? Did he say who'd hired him on?"

"One of the fisheries, down at the point, to keep records," and then he turned and gestured the source of that wispy fish and tide smell. "There are several there but none I've found know anything of my friend, and none are hiring accountants."

"Perhaps your friend Poynter didn't care for his new job and has already left town," I suggested.

"No, no, he wouldn't do that. He was *expecting* me."

My next question seemed the most logical. "Where did he direct you to meet him once you arrived?"

Now Garret pointed to a multi-storied blockhouse across the street. "The motel there, the Hilman House. I took a room–only fifty-cents a night, so I can't complain about *that*–but the strange thing is . . ." He paused though an aggravation. "When I checked myself in, the clerk said that Leonard Poynter, my friend, had indeed rented a room there, and was currently still a guest. The problem is I can't for the life of me find him."

So obvious was Mr. Garret's enigma but now I possessed an enigma of my own. That excited fugue-state came back into my head, and I knew that I'd discovered something for sure. First a town called Olmstead and a character called Olmstead, and now?

In Lovecraft's *The Shadow Over Innsmouth*, the protagonist checks into a motel called the *Gilman* House, and now here I stood looking at a motel called the *Hilman* House. I'm sorry, but *this* was more than coincidence. It *had* to be. Something about this tedious town, without a doubt, impressed Lovecraft enough to at least borrow some names from it, and I was suddenly convinced that there must be more influences waiting to be divulged.

Garret peered close, concern in his eyes. "Mr. Morley? Are you all right?"

His voice snapped me out of my mental revel. "Oh, sorry. Something sidetracked me. But, you know what? I think I'll be staying on for a few days after all."

"Splendid!" He whispered again, through a tight smile. "It'll be good to know that I'm not the only normal person in town."

I laughed distractedly but before I could say more . . .

"Hello, gentlemen," a soft voice greeted.

We both turned to take wide-eyed note of a commonly attired yet perfectly attractive woman. She strolled down the walk, arms full of groceries, and grinned more than typically at the two of us.

Garret tipped his hat. "Miss . . ."

"Gorgeous day, isn't it?" I plodded.

"Oh, yes it is," and that was the extent of our discourse.

"There's a looker," Garret whispered.

"I should say so," I remarked, actually a bit ashamed, for this woman's over-typical good looks gave me cause peer more than I should've. Her bosom could be described as raucous, as she was not only endowed but appeared un-brassier'd. The respect I had for my Christian faith reminded me what Jesus said regarding lust, but not in enough time to avert my eyes.

"As they say in England," chuckled my friend, "there goes the apple-dumpling cart," but then he leaned closer to denote discretion, "but that's another queer thing about this little town."

"That being?"

"I'm serious, man. I've never seen so many pregnant women in one place in my life."

"Preg–" I began, and when I gave myself another yet more distanced glance, the more than moderate gibbosity of the woman's abdomen told all. "Well, I'll be. You seem to be correct."

"Four or five months at least, and it's not the first biscuit in that one's oven, either."

I looked dismayed. "How on earth can you tell *that?*"

He elbowed me with a grin. "You saw the jugs on her. They're still filled up from the last one."

The uncultivated talk was making me uneasy, for it wasn't my bent. "But, really, what did you mean when you said you've never seen so many–"

"This town–I'm serious. I'll bet that's the dozenth pregnant woman I've seen since I've been here, and I'm telling you, most of them have been lookers."

"Really ... Still, it's a good thing, if you don't mind my opinion. The government is wise to encourage propagation since the Spanish Flu epidemic of '18. We lost half a million in that, they say, and almost all of them young men."

Garret nodded grimly. "And right after losing–what?–another hundred-some thousand more men in that devilish war with the Huns. I agree with you. America needs more birthing, especially if we have to get into this next one with Germany, like so many believe."

I wasn't sure how I felt on this subject; I tended to trust authority. "But the President just declared neutrality in the European War."

"It doesn't give me much comfort, I'll tell you. Right after Germany and Russia signed the non-aggression pact, look what happens. Russia invades Finland. And don't believe that Brit Neville Chamberlain either. Peace in our time? Hitler's pulling the wool over the whole world's eyes. And what are the Japanese doing in the meantime? Invading Manchuria."

"Let's pray God that men can find a diplomatic solution." It was my nature not to engage in political conversation, though the man had some points that perhaps gave me cause to feel naive. "But getting back to our previous, if not a bit too earthy topic, we must be fruitful and multiply–"

"Just as it says in the Good Book, yes. And I tell you," he went on, "I'm not too pleased about Congress striking the Comstock Act– when was that? Last year?"

"No, no, it was '36, and we agree again, William. Barrier prophylactics should remain illegal except when prescribed by a physician for the prevention of disease. An open market for such things really does circumvent nature–"

"And God's will, if you don't mind my saying so."

"Not at all," but then we both looked at each other and laughed. "Not exactly everyday conversation, eh?"

"No, my friend, it isn't, but it's still invigorating to find someone who shares my doctrines," he said.

"Likewise. So now I suppose you'll be returning to your search for your friend, Poynter. I'm going to check in to the Hilman and then take a stroll about. I'll be sure to keep an eye out for your friend. Let's meet for dinner tonight. If I happen to find your friend, I'll bring him. Say, seven o'clock?"

"A terrific idea, Mr. Morley–"

"Call me Foster, please. And where's a suitable restaurant?"

Again, he pointed just across the street, to the small restaurant I'd noticed earlier, Wraxall's Eatery. "It's not bad, and large portions for a slight price."

"Good. Seven–I'll see you then."

Garret walked off, a spring in his step now that he had a "normal" confidante. I, on the other hand, had a new exhilaration to feed my Lovecraftian obsession. Though the town looked nothing like the Master's Innsmouth, what little tidbits of recognition might I find in its details?

I fetched my valise from the coach, and when I returned to the street, the driver stood sullenly before me. The look on his face might be called hateful. "Why ya got your bag? We'll be takin' off for Salem now. Ya t'ain't staying in Olmstead now, are ya?"

"Actually, yes," I told him. "I've changed my mind and decided to stay a few days."

At first, he appeared about to object, as though the prospect offended him. After all, I wasn't an "Olmsteader." It occurred to me just now how small his mouth seemed. The little twist of lips turned. "Now's I thinkin' on it, you might like Olmstead." Then the fleshy twist merged into something like a smile. "And Olmstead might like *you.*"

He climbed back aboard the bus, and drove off in a smoke-chugging clatter.

So Olmstead might like me? I mused. Of that I cared little. But clearly something about it had impacted Lovecraft to blend some of its peripheries into his shuddering tale of inbred fish-people and pseudo-occult horror.

Just like in the story, the vested, elderly clerk at the Hilman's front desk seemed pleasant and conventional enough; he was all too happy to let me a room. Without much pre-cognizance, I blurted, "Would a Room 428 be available?" for this–as astute readers will know–was the room Robert Olmstead rented in the story.

"So you've been here before!" the man seemed to delight in a neutral accent. "That can only mean you like our accommodations. See, since the rebuild, Olmstead looks quite nice and's got some fine amenities."

I didn't spoil his assumption by revealing that I'd never previously visited, but instead I evaded by inquiring, "The 'rebuild?'"

"Ah, yes, sir. 1930, '31 thereabouts, government contractors put up all these nice, sturdy block buildings. Fire-proof, storm proof, like they done lots'a places. When the Great Storm hit last September, there weren't no damage at all. But Olmstead of the past was a sorry sight. Just an old rotten wharf town fallin' in on itself. God bless Roosevelt and Garner!"

This came as no surprise. Soon after the stock market collapsed in '28, the Federal Re-Employment Act hired on thousands of jobless for reconstruction purposes, paying a dollar a day. Many towns in disrepair were rebuilt. Now, however, inspired by the new information, I couldn't help but feel sure that what Olmstead looked like before this rebuild *had* to be the visual picture Lovecraft painted for his readers in *The Shadow Over Innsmouth.*

My work's cut out for me, I thought, thrilled by the promise. Certainly, behind Olmstead's new face there must remain some vestiges of its *old* face. I was determined to find the crannies and cracks that would lead me to them.

Room 428 proved quite comfortable: well-furnished, a new bed, even its own bathroom complete with Cannon brand towels. Nothing like the dingy hovel that happenstance had forced Lovecraft's character into. The bathroom, in fact, offered brand new cakes of Lux Toilet Soap, the best national brand. I was also impressed by the RCA Victor Console radio provided as well; it was similar– though not *quite* as fine as the pricier model I owned in Providence. The room's metal-framed windows offered a view of the seaward rise, a formidable sight. If anything unnerved me, it was the room's *newness.* The entire building, in fact, felt barely used, as though it were a facade, feigning an appearance of prosperity that didn't truly exist.

But what an absurd thought!

As I made my exit from the room, I caught sight of a maid leaving another room, but she wasn't pushing the expected cart full of brooms and linens. She was hefting a suitcase. She couldn't be a guest: her outfit left no doubt as to her duties. The scenario simply seemed odd, but what alarmed me right off was her most obvious trait.

She was pregnant.

"Miss!" I called out, rushing down. "You mustn't carry that in your current state! Let me take it for you."

When I'd approached her directly, I was smiled at by a comely, youthful face framed by luxuriant tousles. A more roguish observation might be to say she was one of Garret's "lookers." Shapely legs flexed as she lifted the case, while her gravidness–like the woman on the street--had enhanced her bosom to dimensions that would cause even the most steadfast gentleman to glance more than covertly.

"Oh, that's very kind, sir, but it's not heavy at all," she gently replied.

"I insist. You're with child and shouldn't be carrying–"

"Really, sir." She giggled playfully. "It's light as a feather. And my doctor told me moderate exercise is good for the baby."

I couldn't very well argue. Even pregnant, though, she was strikingly physiqued. She couldn't be much more than twenty, and I guessed her to be late in her term. Something about her proximity to me felt rejuvenating, some impalpable element of her smile, gender, and youth. I considered what she symbolized: vitality, a brimming life blossoming with still more life . . . All which served to remind me of the counter-productivity of my own indulgent existence. Suddenly my mind raced to maintain conversation, if only to continue in her presence a moment more.

"An acquaintance of mine–Mr. Garret–is searching for his friend, a Leonard Poynter. He's apparently taken a room here. Have you had a chance to see him?"

The maid's eyes suddenly seemed weary in spite of her youth and beauty. "No, I'm afraid not, sir," she spoke more quickly now, her full lips glistening. "It's not my place to learn our guests' names."

"Oh, I see," but still I struggled for more to say. "What's your opinion of the menu at the restaurant across the street, miss? I'm to meet Mr. Garret there later."

"Oh, Wraxall's, it's quite good, and Karwell's opens at eight o'clock, if you're one to imbibe since the repeal of Prohibition. The people there are nice. Our little town doesn't seem very big but there's actually a good many folks passing through–workers and salesmen– between the bigger towns and cities."

"That's good to hear, and, yes, it is a nice town indeed–"

"But I really must be going now, sir," she hastened. "It's been pleasant talking to you."

"The pleasure's been all mine . . ."

I watched her turn with a downcast smile, yet couldn't escape the impression that she was slightly uncomfortable.

She disappeared down the stairs, and I urged myself to wait a moment before I proceeded down myself; I couldn't have her thinking I was being a nuisance or worse, caddish. After a minute, however, I entered the stairwell myself. The maid's descending footfalls could be heard echoing in the well; when I peered over the rail, I saw she'd already stopped on the landing and was taking the suitcase through the door. The door's shutting echoed briefly.

Something immediately began to bother me as I took the steps down myself, and I knew what it was when I arrived at the landing she'd stopped at: it was not the lobby door she'd gone into, it was the door to the second floor.

Why would she be taking a guest's suitcase to the second floor?

I tried the knob and found it locked.

A guest had simply changed rooms, I reasoned next. That was all.

Several clerks and presumably a maintenance man busied themselves in the lobby, all quite congenial, and back out on the street now I spied several shop keepers through windows, a fellow sweeping the cobblestoned main road, and a postage carrier. All smiled and nodded to me. When I strolled down the street, still more local persons met my eye, and not one of them failed to speak a greeting or nod cordially. This forced me to recall Garret's observation: *Some odd ones in this town, eh?*

What could he mean by that? Other than the churlish driver and perhaps the several furtive fishermen on the bus, there was nothing at all odd about anyone I'd encountered. He'd mentioned interviewing for jobs at some of the waterfront fisheries; perhaps that's where he'd been treated oddly. Watermen were known to be a sullen and protective lot as a rule.

I'd brought along my copy of *The Shadow Over Innsmouth,* for after a bit of strolling, I was sure I'd want to re-read it, perhaps beneath a shady tree, or in the park if there was one, or maybe the waterfront. It was a copy of the only hardcover of Lovecraft's work to be bound and published in his lifetime, the Visionary Publications edition. It cost one dollar plus postage. I was almost certain now that Lovecraft had indeed been in Olsmstead and had been quite influenced by the place. Knowing this would make the re-reading all the more fascinating.

Now. Find a quiet place to read, I thought.

Across the street, passing a flag circle, a youthful woman bounded by, and she too smiled quite generously at me. Her prettiness equaled that of the maid, but there was another similarity: she, too, was pregnant.

Not that there was anything unseemly about encountering three pregnant women the same day, regardless what Garret believed. It merely seemed coincidental.

Coincidences, though, were the cause of my being here, and when I remembered that, my previous zeal was refreshed. Now I could embark on my quest to uncover more topical parities between this very real town of Olmstead and Lovecraft's very fictitious Innsmouth.

I walked over to the Ethyl Gas Company station, whose sign boasted gasoline for 9 cents per gallon, a penny lower than the city. There I purchased a pack of my favorite Beechies chewing gum with pepsin from a pleasant proprietor but was told that no local maps could be had, just county and state. I was informed, however, that there were benches along the waterfront where I could read comfortably.

A block down, a motion-picture theater advertized Gene Autry's latest: *Prairie Moon.* I now laughed at my fantasies: Lovecraft would've been appalled to find such modern conveniences in the town that was once the model for the crumbling Innsmouth.

Before I could cross the street, engine-roar startled me with some suddenness, and I turned to see a sizable truck rumble by. Its doors read IPSWICH FISH CO., and it was clearly heading north, to its city of provenance. The back of the truck–I could see as it passed–was stacked full with iced-down fish. The anomaly sparked at once: why would a large fishery such as Ipswich be buying fish in Olmstead? *It should be the other way around, shouldn't it?* Olmstead didn't strike me as large nor involved enough to compete with the big fisheries and, besides, the papers made it plain that fishing in this part of Massachusetts had dropped off due to silt disturbance from

27

the Great Storm and higher river salinity caused by the summer's drought.

When a finger tapped me on the shoulder from behind, I flinched and spun. Smiling before me in a work apron and plain cotton dress was a bright-eyed short young woman, no more than thirty. Even more so than the maid, her prettiness radiated, and not even the clumsy workboots and unbecoming hairnet could take from it. The hair seemed caramel-blond beneath the net. "Come in for an ice-cream, sir. They're only five cents, and we make it fresh here. See, we've just got our own machine!"

She seemed to communicate the information with an overflow of pride; I was nearly taken aback when she grabbed my hand outright and gestured me into the shop which only now did I discern to be Baxter's General Store and Postal Annex via stenciled paint on the window-glass.

The bell rang as we passed through. "My name's Mary Simpson, sir," she brimmed and rushed around the counter. "I suppose you're only passing through but you really *must* have an ice-cream."

My amusement was intensified by the aforementioned prettiness. "A chocolate, please. I'm Foster Morley, Miss Simpson, and you're correct, I am just passing through, a bit of a traveling holiday, exploring new parts and such. Plus I'm an avid reader. But I hope to be staying at least several days. I've a room at the Hilman."

"Oh, good. It's a nice motel now, and so is everything else since the rebuild."

"Mmm, yes, so I've been told by the desk clerk . . .," but at once I was seized by an abrupt beguilement: I saw now–now that I'd had chance to make a more definitive visual surveillance–that the bright and bubbly Miss Simpson was not only very attractive and very amply bosomed but also very pregnant. I could detect this quite plainly by the protrusion of her apron. "I'm finding Olmstead most interesting," I continued. "A successful example of President Roosevelt's social refurbishment program."

"Oh, yes, sir. Olmstead was barely fit to live in before that. But now we've got all new buildings, a library, a new warehouse district and fire station; we even have an ice-factory on the waterfront, like what they have in the big ports."

"As a matter of fact, I just saw a truck bound for Ipswich loaded with iced fish. I take it the fishing's in good repair here?"

She passed me my bowl with a spoon. "It's never been better, sir—"

"Please, call me Foster, Mary, and please allow me to buy you an ice-cream as well."

This smidgen of generosity delighted her. "Thank you, sir—er, Foster," and then she fixed a bowl for herself. "But the fishing, yes, it's the backbone of the town. We're actually selling fish to many towns, even Boston, while in the past if we wanted fish, we'd have to buy it from them. Fishing's better here now than anywhere else. In Olmstead, you'd scarcely know there's a depression."

Since she'd made the observation, I suddenly had to agree. I saw only clean streets, fine buildings, and smiling people since I'd arrived, not disheartened breadlines, uncollected garbage, and collapsing homes. In addition, I saw another Lovecraftian parallel: Innsmouth, like Olmstead, was an unusually thriving fishing town.

"See," she continued with her professional pride, pointing her spoon to the shiny white machines. "We have Westinghouse meat-keepers, too, and our own delivery truck that's almost new. And—"

I waited for her to finish but instead her eyes merely widened in silence.

"Is something the matter, Mary?"

"What a coincidence!" she squealed. "Your book, I mean!"

I'd set my copy of *Innsmouth* on the counter when I'd taken the bowl. Her recognition amazed me. "Don't tell me you're a reader of the great H.P. Lovecraft?"

"No, Foster, only because I never learned to read much. I recognize the name because when I was only eighteen, Mr. Lovecraft stayed in Olmstead for a short time."

I very nearly dropped my bowl. "Mary. You didn't happen . . . to *meet* Mr. Lovecraft, did you?"

"Oh, no, I didn't get that privilege, but here's something interesting. Back then, Baxter's was a First National Mart, and my brother, Paul–he was seventeen at the time–he actually waited on Mr. Lovecraft in this very store you're standing in now. Mr. Lovecraft wanted directions about town, so Paul drew him a map."

This shock of shocks almost put my knees out. The attractive woman's brother had *met* the Master! What precious conversation must have taken place. And now this: the reference to her brother's map! Surely this had founded Lovecraft's early scene in the story where a congenial "grocery youth" had provided Robert Olmstead with just that: a *map* of Innsmouth. Like most writers, HPL had used an ordinary factual occurrence in which to dress the fiction.

"Foster, why, you look–"

"Dumbstruck?" I laughed. "It's true, Mary. I know it might seem peculiar but the work of Lovecraft is my foremost hobby; I pursue it with a passion as well as any information about his life in general. And this is such a stroke of luck. You could very well help me in my indulgence. Please allow me to take you and your brother to luncheon sometime. Aside from your wonderful company, of course, I'd just like–Paul, is it?–I'd like to ask him a few questions about Lovecraft's visit–" but then the bungle hit me like a physical blow. "Pardon me, Mary, but of course I meant you, your brother, *and* your husband."

Mary didn't balk at the comment; she merely replied, "Oh, I'm afraid my husband turned out to be not much of one. He left me for another woman, ran off to Maryland."

"I truly regret to hear that, Mary. You deserve better than an irresponsible lout like that." It infuriated me, that any real man could abandon a pregnant wife.

"Oh, it's all right. It's one of life's lessons," came a surprisingly cheerful reply. "My stepfather says the hardest lessons serve us best."

"How true."

"And I *do* have a good life. I have good work and live in a good town. I feel very blessed."

"A selfless and commendable attitude. Too many these days take so much for granted," I amended.

"And my brother, Paul"–her glance cast down for a moment–"he's not well, I'm afraid, and wouldn't be able to manage an outing."

I didn't know how to respond other than topically. "Oh, that's too bad. I hope he recovers quickly."

"But I'd be happy to talk to you about Mr. Lovecraft at any convenience. You see, Paul quite took to the man, and related to me everything they talked about while Mr. Lovecraft was here. "

"Then, please, we must do that, Mary."

She gave the faintest coy smile. "That is if your *wife* doesn't mind you taking another woman to lunch."

"I've never married," I blurted, only now aware of the slightly sticky situation. She was pregnant, after all–with a stumblebum's child.

"You can't be serious!" Came her exclamation after another spoonful of ice cream. "A handsome, well-mannered gentleman like you? *Never* married?"

I prayed I didn't blush. "I fear I wouldn't be suitable for any woman," and then I played it off with a laugh. "I'm far too indulgent."

"Oh, I don't believe that!"

"But, yes, I'll stop in tomorrow morn and you can tell me a time convenient for you."

"That would be fine, Foster. I'll look forward to it."

By now I felt a bit guilty admitting this attraction to a woman with child but, of course, my only interest was strictly of the platonic variety. That aside, this was a great opportunity. What Mary could convey of Paul's conversations with the Master would be of joyous interest to me. I was about to continue conversation when the bell rang again and the door opened.

"Oh, hi, Dr. Anstruther," greeted Mary.

"Hello, my dear . . ."

"Dr. Anstruther, meet Foster Morley. He's here on vacation."

I turned to face a distinguished, well-suited man with iron-grey hair and beard. "How do you do, sir?" I shook a soft but strong hand.

He grinned broadly. "I'm splendid, Mr. Foster. How are you liking our little town?"

"I'm intrigued by it, sir, a very clean, self-respecting prefect, indeed." I glanced minutely to Mary. "And such nice townsfolk."

"Oh, yes. Perhaps you're not aware, but you're sampling the wares of Olmstead's very first ice cream machine. It caused quite a row when it was first installed."

"God bless such luxuries!" I tried to joke.

"We're prospering where other towns are going by the wayside–quite a feat in these economic times. We've been very fortunate of late." He turned to Mary, handing her a stub of paper. "Dear, check this claim number, please. I'm expecting a delivery of some urgency. Mrs. Crommer should be going into labor any day now."

"I completely forgot," Mary remarked, checking a shelf of boxes, then finding one. "Will it be her tenth?"

"Her eleventh," the doctor redressed. He glanced to me. "Stock for the future, as the President says."

"Uh, yes. So true," I practically stammered. But this information? A woman expecting her *eleventh* child? And thus far I'd seen several other expectant mothers. *Olmstead is certainly a virile town . . .*

Mary opened the box on the counter, and Dr. Anstruther withdrew its contents: four securely packed quart bottles of caramel-colored glass. Each was clearly labeled: CHLOROFORM.

"No safer anesthetic for difficult births," Anstruther commented, and replaced the bottles.

"American medical technology," I offered, "seems more burgeoning now than ever before. I've read they'd found a near-cure for schizophrenia, via electric current."

"Not to mention bone-marrow transplantation, for patients with blood problems, and coming breakthroughs against poliomyelitis. America's leading the way by leaps and bounds. Judging by the current global political climate, though, I fear we'll be focusing our prowess of knowledge and industry on war rather than peace."

"Let's pray that's not the case," I said. "This man Hitler does seem sincere in his promise to annex no more land after Austria. Plus there's his pact with the Soviets."

"Time will tell, Mr. Foster. And now, I must go." He shook my hand once more. "I'll hope to see you soon."

"Good day, doctor . . ."

"As fine a small town doctor as you could ever ask," Mary complimented after he left. "Seems what he's doing most of these days is delivering babies. He's delivered all of mine too."

I hoped it wouldn't be too abrupt a departure from good manners to ask, for the question was somehow irresistible. "How many children has God blessed you with, Mary?"

"Nine"–she errantly patted her swollen abdomen–"counting this one."

Nine children, and with no husband to bear half the responsibility, came my regretful thought. Truly, she was a strong woman. "It must be very difficult for you, being on your own, I mean."

"Oh, my stepfather helps out a lot. It's just that he's getting so old now. And, Paul . . . well–"

Suddenly there came a thunk from the back room, and what I could only perceive as an accommodating human grunt. "What's he done now?" Mary whined. "I'll be right back, Foster." She scurried through a door behind her.

I couldn't help but overhear:

"Can't you *wait?*" Mary's muffled voice complained.

"Not-not much longer, I can't." A male voice, one in some distress.

"But there's a nice man out front, and he's asked me to dine with him! Now–" A pause, then what seemed a grunt on her part. "–get back in your chair! You'll just have to wait! I won't be long–"

"I'll try . . ."

Mary returned with a sheepish smile, then came close to whisper, "That was Paul, just trying to get attention, I'm afraid." She seemed to be tempering herself against an inner rage. "The reason it wouldn't do to have you meet him is because of his injuries. He's very self-conscious–he had a terrible accident several years ago."

A selfish notion, I know, but it made me cringe to realize that the true-life model for Lovecraft's "grocery youth" was on the other side of that door and not accessible to me. And what of these injuries? There was no genteel way to inquire.

"I let him stay in the back while I'm working, so he doesn't get too lonely. Sometimes he even sleeps here when no one can give him a drive home."

"Oh, I see. It's, um, good that you can do that," was all I could muster to say, but what else could she have meant by her insistence, *Get back in your chair*–? That and the remark about drives home?

She could only mean a *wheel*chair.

The moment had struck an awkward note but it was that same selfishness of mine that sufficed to turn the subject. "Before I'm on my way, I have a question."

She leaned over, elbows on counter, chin in fists, and smiled in a way that struck me as dreamy, though I couldn't imagine that *my* presence solicited the look. "Ask me anything, Foster. You're really an interesting man."

Did I audibly gulp? I hope not! "I've decided to find a quiet place outdoors to read," and then I held up my book. "See, reading the story whose setting Lovecraft formed by his direct impressions of this very town strikes me as fascinating; it's my favorite story of any, and re-reading it here will allow for an entirely new perception."

"I think I know what you mean," she said. "But the Olmstead you're seeing today is nothing alike what Mr. Lovecraft saw when he was here so many years ago."

"That's my point!" I exclaimed of her perceptivity. "Would you by chance have a photograph of Olmstead before the rebuild? I'd love to compare it to Lovecraft's descriptions in the book."

"We've never had a camera, but . . ." She held a finger up. "There is a man you could try talking to. Er, well, maybe that's not such a good idea."

Was she teasing me now? I absolutely *quailed*. "Mary, I implore you, please–"

"There's a townsman who used to be a photographer; he trained in New York even, and took pictures for newspapers. He even took a picture of Mr. Lovecraft standing on the New Church Green with Paul. You can see the entire waterfront in the background, the harbor inlet and lighthouse, the old Larsh Refinery, and the town dock, which they used to call Innswich Point back then."

I could've collapsed by these new parallels! Innswich: obviously a variation of Innsmouth. The dead lighthouse which overlooked the notorious *Devil's* Reef from whence came the batrachian Deep Ones. And the Larsh Refinery: in Lovecraft's grand tale, it was at the *Marsh* Refinery where the gift of gold trinkets bestowed to human worshipers by the Deep Ones was melted down and sold on the market. *I MUST see that picture!* I determined.

"Please, Mary. How can I find this photographer? It's imperative, truly–"

Her chin slumped in her palms. "How can I say no to *you*? I only mean that it's not a good idea. The man's name is Cyrus Zalen. He's about forty but he looks sixty, and you can' miss him. He always wears the same long greasy black raincoat. He smells horrible and he's . . . well, he's just not nice. He lives at the poorhouse behind the new fire station."

Cyrus Zalen. Presumably a breadliner or, to use Lovecraft's term, a "loafer." In Providence, they called them "bums" and "rummies."

"An unfortunate turn of fate for a newspaper photographer," I remarked.

"He was a fine photographer . . . before he got mixed up with the heroin. In New York he got hooked up with ex-soldiers who'd become addicted to it when they went on leave in France, a city called . . . Marcy? I can't remember."

"Marseilles," I corrected. I'd read of these places there called heroin laboratories where they converted the resin from opium poppies into this devastating new drug. "Still, I'll have to find Mr. Zalen."

The prospect seemed to worry her. "Please don't, Foster. He's not a nice man. He'll try to connive money out of you, and he may even be a thief. He's known to do . . . immoral things, but it would be unladlylike for me to explain. And this was so many years ago, at least ten, I guess. I'm sure he doesn't have the photo anymore anyway. Really, Foster, don't go there." She leaned even closer. "It's a *dirty* place where he lives–there's probably diseases. A woman died of typhus there several years ago."

I didn't take her warning lightly, actually flattered by her concern for my well-being. But if it was money that Mr. Zalen wanted for his old pictures, then money he would have. My wallet was chock full.

"You needn't worry, Mary. I'm of hardy enough stock. I survived the outbreaks of 1919 and 1923, and, in fact, I've not been sick a day in my life. I'll be very careful when interviewing Mr. Zalen, and I can't thank you enough for your guidance."

She gripped my forearm with some determination. "At least make a deal with me, Foster. I think Paul has an extra copy of the photo. If so, I'll get it for you, if you promise *not* to go to Cyrus Zalen's."

I was touched to the point of amusement by the vigor with which she insisted I not meet this man. "All right, Mary. I promise."

She beamed a smile, then gave me a sudden hug which almost made me flinch. The all too brief contact brought my cheek to hers. The scent of her hair was luxuriant.

"And I can't thank you enough," I went on, "for your acceptance of my invitation for luncheon tomorrow. Oh, and here–for your wonderful ice cream." I put five-dollars on the counter.

"But it's only five cents–"

"Keep it, please. You can buy a special treat for your stepfather and children."

The moment lengthened. Her eyes held on mine. "You're very nice, Foster," she gushed. "Thank you . . ."

"Until tomorrow, then!" and I was off.

I left in a blissful rush, not only quite taken by the cherubic and lovely girl but also by this new and surprising kindle to my obsession.

I knew at once that I must break the promise I'd made. Her concern was obviously exaggerated, and I couldn't very well deprive her brother of a photograph that must mean a great deal to him. *The poorhouse behind the new fire station,* I recalled, and– there! A sign right before me read FIREHOUSE with an arrow pointing west. A sudden uproar startled me, when several more fish-laden trucks hauled around the cobblestoned circle, but when they passed I noticed that the westernmost road entry was cordoned off and closed–sewerpipe workers were digging–so I thought it best to cut around behind the row of block buildings that housed Baxter's General Store, Wraxall's Eatery, and the others. The alleyway gave wide birth and I was pleased to find it clean, free of garbage and its attendant stench, and absent of vermin. I was halfway along, though, when I heard a voice so wee I thought it must be my imagination.

I stopped, listened . . .

"Bugger. You did that on purpose. I *know* you did. You want to mess things up for me."

True, the voice was oh-so-faint but unmistakably the voice of Mary, and when I turned I noticed a narrow window opened just a crack.

It was not my nature at all–please, believe me--but something connatural in my psyche *forced* my eyes to that crack . . .

Time seemed to freeze when my vision fully registered the macabre scene within. A thin, haggard man sat troubled in a wheelchair–Paul, no doubt. Either age or despair ran lines down his face like a wood-carver's awl; his hair was a shaggy tumult. But the severity of his overall physical state trivialized the ramshackled appearance and uncleanliness.

I felt wounded appraising him . . .

His legs ended at the knees, leaving sleeves of empty denim.

His arms ended at the elbows.

My God, I thought. I'd never imagined that the accident Mary referred to could've been so calamitous. My spirit was left tamped when the thought impacted me: that this ruined twig of a man had just over a decade ago been the energetic seventeen-year-old "grocery youth" who'd generously prepared Lovecraft/Robert Olmstead with a hand-drawn map of the town.

And what was now taking place was a pitiable site, indeed.

The girth of Mary's belly made it difficult for her to bend over, yet bend over she did, after fiddled at Paul's trousers. It was clear now what his problem had been earlier. A bucket in the corner of the office told me that's where he'd been struggling to when he'd flopped himself out of the chair: for the purpose of urinating, a task not easily accomplished given his disabilities. I could only presume that his trousers were left perpetually open for such emergencies.

Distaste plainly stamped on her face, Mary held a tin can betwixt the poor man's legs, into which he now voided his bladder.

Her wince intensified. "For goodness sake, Paul! You go more than a horse! Hurry!"

Another full minute lapsed when finally the void terminated and Mary aversively emptied it in the small sink. "You just want attention anytime you know I'm getting some."

"I do not," he said forlornly. "I had to go and you weren't here."

She sat with some effort in a fold down chair, cradling the distended belly. "I'm doing all of this for you and step-dad, you know. Working two jobs and carrying another baby. I'm tired of you taking me for granted. You're lucky to be alive, you know, and you *wouldn't* be, Paul, if it weren't for me."

Paul railed, elevating his stumps. "Oh, yeah, I'm so lucky to be alive! Thanks very much!"

"Don't talk like that," she said in a lower and somehow darker tone. "We could have it a lot worse. Both of us."

"He wanted to talk to *me,* not *you,*" Paul objected, spittle on his lips and tears in his eyes. "I knew Lovecraft better than you, and just because–"

"That's enough," came her tempered retort, then she rose from the chair, but before she could exit–

"Mary, wait! Please!" the invalid implored.

"What?" she nearly growled.

"I need you to . . ."

"You need me to *what?*"

Now his voice degraded to a pitiful peep "You know . . . With your hand..."

A hot glare raged on her face. "No! It's dirty and sinful! It's disgusting!"

My brows rose high.

Paul's forlorn whine continued. "But it's so hard to do it myself. I get lonely back here, and . . ."

"No!"

"At least-at least . . . can I see? I've got nothing else, Mary. Please. Let me see, just for a second . . ."

Mary's comely visage was now a mask of disdain. "No! I'm your sister, for goodness sake!" then she left the room in a whir and slammed the door.

First, the blaring sight, then, second, the implications, left me agog at the window. Yet when my eyes fond their way back to the unfortunate Paul, I heard my very soul groan . . .

He sat now in a desperate hunch, his back to me, his shoulders moving as his forlorn whimpers drew on. I did not need to see to know that he was attempting to masturbate with his elbow stumps.

What a tragedy, I thought.

My secret gaze retreated. Though the situation offended my outer sensibilities, I did not issue judgments, but what a sorry plight life left to so many. *The poor girl, pregnant while having to work two jobs to support an invalid brother and most likely an invalid stepfather. While the poor brother himself has only . . . this as his only accessible mode of pleasure.* The grim reality only served to reflect more of myself back into whatever sense of self-awareness I possessed. I was the indulgent, filthy rich, having never had to work in my life, while these people.

I knew that before I left this town, I would do something quite generous for this destitute family . . .

The alley's exit conducted me to a crossroad, when I turned westward and followed the sign. Clean block buildings lined one side of the street, stands of dense trees lined the other. I set my quiet despair behind me, to re-attended my task.

I MUST locate this Cryus Zalen . . .

Sunlight sifted through high branches while from the east a gentle surf touched my ears. I wondered if Lovecraft had ever walked this particular street and so hoped that he had. I knew that I was seeing what he saw as his mind worked on the pieces of *The Shadow Over Innsmouth.*

A crunch to my left stopped my gait. I turned, scanned the crush of trees, but saw no one where I was sure someone must be. The sound I'd heard was unmistakable: a footstep crunching down on the drought-withered detritus of the woods.

After several more paces, the crunch resounded again.

"Hello there!" I called when I saw the figure shamble through the trees. A figure, yes, adorned in a long, ruined black raincoat. "Mr. Zalen! Please! I've dire need to speak with you!"

The figure disappeared as quickly as if it were part of the woods.

I could only wonder now just how debilitated Mr. Zalen had become via the rigors of opiate addiction and impoverishment. The latter stages of such misfortunes regularly left its victims incoherent or fully mad. Should this be the case with Zalen, my trek could well prove pointless.

A ten-minute stroll left me standing before the new fire station where several men chatted amiably while they washed and polished the grand, new pumper truck. Not half a block on, I found what could only be the poorhouse.

The single-floored length of small apartments looked pressed down by adversity, as though soullessness were as salient a feature as the compartments' peeling paint and rag-stuffed broken window panes. From them issued the smells of urine and rotting food. An elderly man sat slumped and glassy-eyed before one dingy-doored room, to the effect that I thought he might be deceased until he shivered once, and hacked. An obese blind woman with a white cane sat just as dejected at the next unit. She looked up sightlessly when she'd no doubt heard my passing, then rose from the milk crate she used for a chair, tapped back to the doorway, and went in. The door slammed.

The end unit struck me as darker than all the rest, though the sunlight here shone evenly across the entire length of apartments. A doorless postal box revealed no occupant's name, and I noticed a grease-stained garbage bag sitting roadside filled with stubs of burned down candles, expended flash bulbs, and empty food cans aswarm with flies. A cracked walkway led me forward until I stopped, forced to eye a curious door-knocker mounted in the beaten door's center stile, a queer oval of tarnished bronze depicting a morose half-formed face. Just two eyes, no mouth or nose, no additional features.

I wrapped hesitantly with the knocker, staring uneasily at the name plaque posted just above: C. ZALEN.

3

Whatthe door opened to show me was more of what I expected: a thin, pallid man demonstrating every sign of physical squalor. He still wore the ruinous black raincoat, which hung open to show him shirtless, sunken-chested, slat-ribbed. Frayed trousers torn off at the knees were what he wore below the waist, as well as rotten shoes. His already sunken eyes appeared nearly non-existent by the smudge-like crescents beneath them. I made every attempt to smile and seem unfazed.

"Ah, Mr. Zalen. My name is Foster Morley. I saw you cutting home through the woods but I guess you didn't hear me."

The man frowned. Longish black hair had been slicked back off his brow by either tonic or, more likely, the natural oils from his scalp that had accreted from not washing often. "What do you want?" he asked in a voice that sounded more hardy than I would expect from such a dilapidated unfortunate.

"You're the photographer, correct? The newspaper man, or have I been informed in error?"

"That was a lifetime ago, but I guess if you've been *informed* about me, you're either police or a client . . . and you don't look like police so I guess you better come in."

So he must still have some clients for his photography business, I reckoned. Which meant he had *some* money coming in. He invited me inside to a living room in worse repair than the exterior: a legless couch, the sparsest furniture, and one of those large wooden cable spools on end, to serve as a table. A chemical scent in the air suggested the solutions of photo development. Before he closed and bolted the door, he peeked both ways outside, as if suspicious of something. He oddly reached *behind* a bookcase whose shelves dipped at their centers, and withdrew a simple folder.

"Fifty cents each, Mr. Morley," he told me, and handed me the folder. "I can tell by the way you dress you're not on the outs like a lot of folks these days. You want to buy, not sell."

I couldn't imagine what he meant but I could tell by viewing the folder's side what it contained: a hefty stack of photographs. An instantaneous thrill made my nerves buzz at the prospect. Mary, even in her disapproval of the man, must've called ahead to tell him what it was I sought. I nervously took a seat, and flung open the folder . . .

What a horror the times have turned this world into. I could've gagged at the repellent images that leapt up at my eyes from the glossy surfaces of the photographs. These were neither pictures of Lovecraft nor of Olmstead in days past. It was, instead, outright pornography.

The scenes depicted in the few sheets I looked at need not be described. I can only say that the photography itself was strikingly vivid and every bit of expert.

"But the ones with the white girl making it with the colored fellas are a buck each," he continued. He skimmed off the tattered raincoat and hung it up on a nail in the wall. "If you're into kids, they're two bucks each."

I thrust the evil folder back to him. "This is . . . not . . . what I came for."

"Oh, so you're a seller? Well, you gotta pay me up front for the film and developer, and I get half of what I can sell 'em for. But keep in mind, if they ain't pretty enough, I won't bother 'cos I can't sell the pictures. And the more you can talk 'em into doing, the more I can sell 'em for."

Through a dazedness of incomprehension, I merely replied, *"What?"*

He shot me a glare sharp as a dagger. "It's the business, man! You got a couple cute daughters and you want me to snap 'em nude or fuckin' guys, right?"

I stared. "No," I croaked. "I have no children."

"Then what do you want, Morley?" he suddenly yelled. "I need *money,* and you're wasting my time! Get out of here!"

Bleary-eyed, I gave him a ten-dollar bill.

"What's the sawbuck for?" his rant continued after snapping the bill from my fingers. "I don't turn tricks, man! I'm no swish! You want to fuck a *girl,* fine, I got one here, but don't bullshit around! You're starting to scare the shit out of me–" and then he yelled at what was presumably the door to the bedroom. "Candace! Come out here!"

Before I could object, the door opened, and out stepped a timid and very naked woman in her twenties. One hand covered her bare pubis; her other arm attempted to cover two very swollen breasts. What she couldn't cover at all, however, was the belly stretched out tight and huge from a state of pregnancy that had to be close to the end of its term. Obliquely, I made out a radio tune from the other room, "Heaven Can Wait," I believe, by Glen Gray.

The girl smiled crookedly at me through a gap in the hair falling over her face. "Hi. We-we could have a nice time together, sir . . ."

More of the real world I didn't care for at all. By now I'd managed the shock of this horrendous miscalculation, and produced a frown of my own which I directed immediately to Zalen. "I gave you the money so you needn't feel your valuable time is *wasted.* I'm not interested in prostitution nor pornography."

Zalen chuckled. "Come on, Mr. Morley. You ever had your tallywhacker in a *pregnant* girl? Bet'cha haven't."

"You're a profane vagabond!" I yelled at him.

"–and it's not like you can knock her up."

I wished that looks could kill at that moment, for my look of utter loathing would surely have shorn him in half. "I'm interested in a *particular* photograph I'm told you're in possession of, and if this is the case, I'll pay you one hundred more dollars for it."

Zalen looked agape at my words, then flicked a hand at the girl, to shoo her back into the bedroom. "A *hundred dollars,* you say?"

"One hundred dollars." Now I noticed what first appeared to be splotches of pepper inside the man's elbows but my naivety wore off in a moment and told me they were needle scars. "My patience is growing thin, Mr. Zalen. Do you or do you not have a photograph of a writer by the name of Howard Phillips Lovecraft?"

For the first time Zalen actually smiled. The couch creaked when he sat down and crossed his thin, white legs. "I remember him, all right. Had a voice like a kazoo, and all the guy ever ate were ginger snaps." He jumped up quickly, and slipped something from the bookcase. He showed it to me behind his gap-toothed smile.

It was a copy of the Visionary Publications edition of *The Shadow Over Innsmouth.*

I removed mine from my jacket pocket and showed him likewise.

"I didn't think anybody even *read* that guy, but I'll tell you, after this came out, a *lot* of folks did, and they weren't too happy with what he had to say about our town. Most of Olmstead back then was moved down to Innswich Point, so the guy changes the name to *Innsmouth.* Christ. Changed all the names but only a little, you know? Like he *wanted* us to know what he was really writing about."

"For God's sake, Mr. Zalen," I countered. "He merely used his topical impressions of this town as a setting for a fantasy story. You're practically accusing him of libel. All writers do things like that." I cleared my throat. "Now. Do you have the photograph?"

"Yeah, I got it, but only the negative. I can have it developed for you tomorrow." His smile turned slatternly. "But I'll take the hundred up front."

I am not a man given to confrontation or brusqueness, but this I would not stand for. "You'll take *five* dollars for processing fees, and the remaining ninety-five when I have what I want," I told him and thrust him another five.

He took it all too eagerly. "Deal. Tomorrow, say four." His eyes turned to cunning slits. "Who told you I had the picture?"

"A friend of mine," I snapped. "A woman named Mary Simpson—"

An abruptitude pushed him back in his seat; he nearly howled. "Oh, now I get it! She's a *friend* of yours, huh? I guess you're not the goodie-two-shoes I pegged you as."

I winced at the remark. "What on earth do you mean?"

"Mary Simpson used to be the town slut. Now, this town was *full* of sluts but Mary took the cake. She was a *whore*, Mr. Morley, a whore of the first water, as my grandfather used to say."

"You're lying," I replied with immediacy. "You're merely trying to incense me because you're resentful of people with means. I see your frowsy smile, Mr. Zalen, but I've a mind to wipe it right off your face by canceling any further business with you and seeing my way out of this den of drugs and iniquity you call your home."

"But you won't do that, *Mr.* Morley, because guys like you always get what they want. You'll be back tomorrow, and you'll have the rest of the money. You just don't want to know the truth."

"And what truth is that?"

"Not too many years ago? Mary Simpson was the top dog dockside whore in all of Innswich. Christ, she's had, like, eight or ten trick babies, man. She made a lot of money for me."

Now it was my turn to smile at the bombast. "I'm supposed to believe you're her panderer? Er, what do they call them now? Pimps?"

"Not is, was. About five years ago the bitch got all high-falutin' on me."

"I still don't believe you. She enlightened me of her plight, regarding her husband who abandoned her. Certainly, the man was of less repute even than you."

"Husband, Jesus." He shook his head with the same grin. "If you believe that, you probably believed that *War of the Worlds* broadcast last October."

Of course, I hadn't believed a word of it; I'd read the book! But for what Zalen was inferring now? *It's just more of his loser's game,* I knew. "And now I suppose you're going to tell me she was a drug addict, like you."

"Naw, she never rode the horse, she was just crazy for cock." He raised a brow. "Well, cock and money."

"And this I'm supposed to take on the authority of a drug addict who would stoop so low as to sell pictures of innocent young pregnant women to degenerates."

"There are a lot of 'degenerates' in the world, Morley. Supply and demand–*there's* what your capitalism's caused." He looked directly at me. "You'd be surprised how many sick fellas there are out there who like to look at pregnant girls."

"And you're the purveyor–to support your narcotics habit, no doubt," I snapped. "Without the supply, there becomes no demand, and then morality returns. But this will never happen as long as predators such as yourself remain in business. You sell desperation, Mr. Zalen, via the exploitation of the subjugated and the poverty-stricken."

This seemed to ruffle a feather or two. "Hey, you're just a rich pud, and you got no right to make judgments about people you don't know. Not everybody's got it easy like you do. The government's building *battleships* for this new Naval Expansion Act while half the country's starving, *Mr.* Morley, and while ten million people got no jobs. Redistribution of wealth is the only moral answer. What an apathetic military industrial complex forces me, or the girl in the back room, or Mary, or *anyone else* to do to survive is nothing *you* have the right comment on."

An unwavering sorrow touched me with the self-admission that, on this particular point, he was correct. Perhaps that's why his truth urged me to despise him all the more. Though obviously a proponent of Marx and Ingles, Zalen had quite accurately labeled me. *A rich pud.* I didn't bother to point out my many acts of philanthropy; I'm sure an alienist in this day and age would diagnose my acts of charity as merely attempts to alleviate guilt. Eventually I replied, "I apologize for any such judgments, but for nothing else. Even if what you accuse Mary of is true, I could hardly blame her, for reasons you've already stated. I believe that she and millions of other downtrodden . . . and even *you*, Mr. Zalen, are essentially victims of an invidious environment."

"Oh, you're a real treat!" he laughed.

I knew I must not let him circumvent me, for that would only refresh my despair, in which case he would win. "I'm here for business regarding my pastime. Let us stick to that. I'll also pay–say, five dollars apiece–for any quality photographs of this Innswich Point that you may have taken before the government renewal effort."

His insolent grin returned, and that cocksure slouch. "You *sure* that's all you want, Mr. Morley?"

"Quite," I asserted.

"But, why? Back then, all of Olmstead, especially the Point, was a slum district."

"Though I'd never expect you to understand, I've an interest in seeing the town as Lovecraft saw it, when it sparked the creative conception for his masterpiece."

"So that's your *hobby*, huh?" he mocked.

"Yes, and one, I'd say, quite harmless when compared to yours."

He laughed. "Don't knock *my* hobby, Mr. Morley. You know, pretty soon I'll have to take a bang." He slapped the inside of an elbow. "You should stick around to watch. It'd do someone like you good to see something like that, to look real hard right into the face of the only salvation that capitalism and all its hypocrisy leaves the poor."

"Stop blaming your weakness on the American economic program," I scoffed at him.

"And this book–" He held up *Innsmouth* again. "Pretty damn stupid if you ask me."

"The likes of you would probably say the same of 'The Rime of the Ancient Mariner,' Mr. Zalen."

He clapped in amusement. "Now you're talkin'! Coleridge was a junkie too! But Lovecraft's *Innsmouth* tripe? He got the town all wrong."

"It wasn't about the *town*," I nearly yelled back. "It was an intricate and very socially symbolic *fantasy.*"

"And he should've at least done a better job changing peoples' names."

I sat up more alertly. "Why do you say that? I thought it mostly the names of *places* he altered."

"No, no, damn near everyone in town he insulted with all that. Remember the bus driver from the story, Joe Sargent? The real man's name was Joe *Major,* for God's sake. And the town founders, the Larshes, he changed to the Marshes. And then there's always Zadok Allen. What did Lovecraft call him? A 'hoary tippler'?"

"Zadok Allen was the piece's most preeminent stock character, a 96-year-old alcoholic who knew all of Innsmouth's darkest secrets."

Another grinning stare. "You're not very perceptive, are you? The real man's name was Adok Zalen. Does that last name ring any bells?"

The implication astounded me. "Zadok Allen-Adok Zalen, and . . . your name, too, is Zalen."

"Yeah, he was my grandfather. Lovecraft got him drunk near the docks one night with some rotgut he bought at the variety store behind the speakeasy. My grandfather died the next day–of alcohol poisoning from the booze your hero Lovecraft gave him."

Could this be true? And if so, it begged the further question: how much of Lovecraft's invention might be the actual invention of Adok Zalen?

"Did the world a favor, though," Zalen prattled on. "Christ, my grandfather was older than the hills and not worth a shit. He was a liar and a thief, and it was time for him to go."

"I commend you for the respect you have for your relatives," I said with a thick sarcasm.

"Lovecraft was a hack. Seabury Quinn was a *much* better writer."

I could've hemorrhaged! "He was nothing of the sort, Mr. Zalen!" My shout of objection sounded near-hysterical, for now Zalen's deliberate hectoring was taking its toll. This was my literary idol, after all, and I would not stand to hear his name and talents sullied by this denizen pornographer. "Now do you have the pictures of the old town or do you not?"

"I got 'em. Wait here," and he got up and loped into the back room.

The nerve of him, I thought, truly riled now. What could *he* know about quality fantasy fiction? The more I speculated, the more I preferred to dismiss his accusation that Lovecraft may have contributed to Adok Zalen's demise. *He's simply asserting these lies for the purpose of a negative effect.* No different from his lies about Mary.

I nearly moaned when my stray glance showed me a slice of the bedroom. He'd left the door open, and what I first noticed was a large-format camera on a tripodular stand. And then . . . something else . . .

Sitting awkwardly on an unsheeted bed was the pregnant prostitute–Candace, I believe he'd called her. She remained naked, and the mammarian effect of her pregnancy had stretched her areolae to pale pink circles. The great, gravid belly only added to the difficulty of what she was doing . . .

A cord girded her upper arm, to distend the veins at her elbow's apex, and into such a vein she was now injecting something through an eyedropper fitted with a hollow needle. *The devil of a man's got her addicted as well, to maintain his exploitation of her . . .*

Zalen, though rummaging out of view, could easily be heard. "You're doing too much," he complained to the girl. "It'll ball up the kid. Remember what happened to Sonia?"

"But I can't help it!" she whined.

"If that kid comes out dead, you're in a world of trouble . . ."

I didn't even *want* to conjecture what he might mean by such a statement. They probably planned to sell the baby to an adoptionage.

The scenario and its implications were sallowing my spirit. I was *not* in my element, and I hoped this would be a lesson to me.

Reappearing, he pulled the door closed behind him, bearing another manila folder. "All I had were these five, *Mr.* Morley," he continued to impudently emphasize. "But it's a hundred for the lot. Take it or leave it."

"I won't be extorted, *Mr.* Zalen," I assured him. Such leverage was to be expected, though. Now that he knew *my* addiction, he would seek as much remuneration as my indulgence would tolerate. "I said five apiece, so it'll be five apiece, and that's *only* if they're precisely what I'm looking for."

"If you like 'em, then pay me what you feel they're worth. How's that?"

"Fair enough," and then I opened the folder.

The first photograph took the wind out of me: a seaward panorama of the town which showed a declining sweep of sagging gambrel rooftops, half-collapsed gables, and smokeless chimney pots. Closer to the sea rose a triad of lofty steeples, two of which were missing their clockfaces. *My God,* I thought. *It's nearly straight from the text: Robert Olmstead's first glimpse of Innsmouth from Joe Sargent's bus window.* A second photo depicted the crumbling waterfront, its half-fallen wharves, fishing boats with ruptured hulls, and mountains of disused lobster traps. A row of sullen factories and processing plants–long abandoned–rose behind this scene of decrepitude and neglect, but again, it was straight from HPL's grimly vivid description in the book. The third photograph showed a low-roofed stone building surrounded by Doric pillars; its outer walls looked eroded by age. Two large double lancet doors stood open, showing depthless black.

"That's the old Freemason Hall," Zalen informed.

And then it hit me. "Of course! It was this building that Lovecraft fancied the Esoteric Order of Dagon, where the crossbred priests held services of worship. They wore flamboyant raiments and tiaras of gold."

"Now turn to the last picture," he goaded.

But the next photo would be the fourth, and I'd thought Zalen said that *five* comprised the lot. Nevertheless, I turned to the next and was stunned by the vision of a macabre sunset over the harbor inlet. The effect made the water look molten. Past more decayed wharves and flanks of leaning, boarded-up shacks whose roofs looked fit to fall in was a vista of the sun-touched channel and what barely noticeably existed a mile or so beyond: an irregular black line just above the water's surface. A dead lighthouse seemed to look northward.

"Lovecraft's Devil's Reef," I knew at a glance.

"Um-hmm. Nothin' devilish about it, though," Zalen said. "It's not really even a reef. It's just a sandbar." He rubbed his hands together. "But they're good pictures, right?"

"They are," I admitted. "It's a pity how you've chosen to vitiate and hence debauch such a laudable talent for the art of photography."

I still felt rocked by the impact of the photos–the truth that they assured in their depiction of the town so long ago. "When, exactly, were these taken, Mr. Zalen?"

"Summer of 1928, July, I'm pretty sure. The only reason I took them was because Lovecraft wanted them. I did it gratis because I thought maybe he'd recommend me to some of those freaky pulp magazines he wrote for. Never did, though, the cheap bastard."

Knowing this even spurred my interest to a new height and as such they were worth considerably more than five dollars apiece. But I was offended by this attempt at extortion. "I'll give you fifty dollars for the set, but not one hundred."

"It's a hundred," he stood firm. Then came that frowzy smile again. "But you haven't seen the last picture, *Mr.* Morley."

"Oh. That's right." I flipped to the final photograph.

I stared down, unblinking. Many seconds ticked by like this. Then I closed the folder, rose, and gave Zalen a hundred-dollar bill. "Good day, Mr. Zalen."

"Tomorrow at four, then?"

"Rest assured I'll be here."

"With another hundred for the Lovecraft picture."

"Another *ninety-five*." I headed for the door. "Please don't disappoint me, Mr. Zalen."

He laughed. "They only way I could do that is if I shoot up a hot shot tonight with the horse I'm gonna buy with the cash you just gave me. Leading cause of death for junkies, you know."

"If you're going to die via an overdose, Mr. Zalen, please don't do it by tomorrow." My hand found the dirty doorknob. "But the day *after* tomorrow would be fine."

"That's the spirit!"

I stepped out of the fetid, chemical-smelling room and felt welcomed into the overly warm light of day. Zalen's squalid apartment had been as dark as his heart.

His near-emaciated form hung in the doorway. "Going back to your room now, huh? To pursue your *hobby?*"

Even in light of what I'd just purchased, the implication via his tone couldn't have offended me more. "My hobby, Mr. Zalen, as you know, is the work of H.P. Lovecraft."

"Right. So I guess you'll walk around town now . . . to *see* what Lovecraft saw."

"That's precisely what I'm going to do, not that it's any of your business. I'm going to Innswich Point."

"It's pretty dull now, Mr. Morley. Just block buildings and a cement pier." Did he snigger? "But don't go there at night."

I frowned on his moss-blotched front step. "Really, Mr. Zalen. The Deep Ones will get me? The acolytes of Barnabas Marsh will offer me up to Dagon?"

"Nope, but the rummies and fugitives will have a lot of fun with a guy like you. Drug runners hole up there."

"Good friends of yours, no doubt."

"They bring it in by boats." The ungainly man scratched the inside of an elbow. "And my grandfather wasn't lying when he told Lovecraft about the network of tunnels under the old waterfront.

They go back to the 1700s. Privateers and smugglers would use them as hideouts."

This was of interest, though I didn't let on.

"And if you want a real treat, take a hike up the main road north and have a look at Mary's place," he snidely continued. "It's a real *slice of life*. It's just shy of the Onderdonks."

My wince communicated my inconvenience, but suddenly I *was* curious, as to where Mary lived in her life of travail and the burden of so many children she was raising all without the help of a man. "Onderdonks," I repeated. "Oh, the roadside stand I saw?"

"Yeah. And try the barbeque," though this time, I wasn't sure how to decipher his belligerent tone of voice.

I was determined to leave now; I would allow no further badgering but as I commenced, he added, "And you might want to read that book a little more closely, too."

I turned on the cracked walk. "Surely you don't mean *The Shadow Over Innsmouth.*"

"What did you think?"

"I've read it dozens of times, Mr. Zalen, with great attentiveness. I can likely quote most of its 25,000 words verbatim, so whatever do you mean?"

The sun highlighted the coarse details of this utterly corroded man. "In the story, what happened to outsiders who did too much nosing around, *Mr.* Morley?"

I walked away, almost amused now by this final, cheap attempt at melodrama.

"And tonight?" he called after me, "when you're fucking Mary for a couple of bucks? Tell her the father of her third or fourth kid says hi . . ."

So much for my amusement. The man was intolerable, and perhaps he was working on my psyche with a bit more effect than I'd care to admit. The only thing I hated more than him was what his manipulation had caused me to do.

When I found a secluded recess of trees, I opened the folder and looked at that fifth picture beneath the photos of the town. It was a photograph of Mary, of course, in depressingly expert resolution and lighting. She was naked, yes, and–worse–pregnant, yet even in this state she managed a gracile posture for Zalen's wretched lens. It was some horrendous collision of opposites that had triggered my instantaneous purchase. But I *knew,* I knew for the life of me and for the love of *God,* that I WAS NOT one of Zalen's degenerate clients. It was the shock of the aforementioned collision that forced me to buy it: loveliness wed to a revolting design, the grace of beauty hand in hand with the balefulness of womanhood subjugated. It occurred to me now that Mary was so beautiful, I could've cringed. I would've guessed her to be five years younger in the picture but if anything her current beauty shined even more intensely. So what if a portion of Zalen's salacious slander was, in essence, fact? Even if, in dimmer times, she *had* been a prostitute, who was I to judge?

I would *not.* For time immemorial, women have been exploited within the grips of a man's lustful world; Mary's past deeds mattered none to me, because I know that God forgives all. I could only pray that He would forgive *me.*

Back toward the town's center, I found a bargain shop which had precisely what I needed: a small briefcase. I made my purchase from yet another amiable Olmsteader, a Mr. Nowry, who was very gracious over my tip. "Where might I find the most direct route to the waterfront?" I asked.

"Just follow the main cobble out front, sir," he pointed. "That'll take ya straight to the water. And a beautiful waterfront it is."

"Yes, I'm certain, and thank you."

"Just make sure," he rushed to add, "you're not there after dark."

The kind warning didn't set well. "But Olmstead hardly seems–"

"Oh, yes, sir, it's a fine town'a fine people. But any town, mind ya, has got its bad apples."

True enough. Before I left, I noticed whom I presumed must be

58

his wife in a back office, scribbling on papers.

Her overlarge frock-dress made no secret of the fact she was pregnant.

Another woman with child, I thought, and I tried with difficulty at first to cogitate my concern. True, I'd encountered what seemed to be an undue number of pregnant women in the little time since I'd arrived, but then I had to remind myself I was essentially a cosmopolite in a new and quite blue collar little village. In truth, I supported the government's initiatives to encourage population-growth. These small townships were more close-knit and, obviously, more conceptive, which was all for the greater good in the long run. Remembering this, I reconsidered my initial reaction to the number of expectant mothers I'd seen. Surely, it was not as *undue* as I'd thought.

As I leisurely approached the waterfront, though, I noticed a short open blockhouse in which I could see a full dozen women contentedly shucking and canning fresh oysters. Most of them were pregnant.

Zalen's assessment of the town's industrial hub rang too true. I saw at once, in spite of the gorgeous, surf-scented vista of the harbor, that Innswich Point was indeed a very dull sight to behold. But, oh, to have seen it as Lovecraft did! At least Zalen's photo would allow me a facsimile of the privilege. Now all that remained was the partial name that the Master had borrowed. More disappointment struck me when I gazed out to the reef but then recalled that it was no reef at all but a ho-hum sandbar. Workers about the Point's many fish processors and boat docks were mainly strong, plain-faced men, much like the few I'd shared the bus with. I wouldn't say that they glared at me, but their cast was not particularly welcoming. This, for sure now, was the impetus for Garret's condemnation of the male populace; he was referring to these surly watermen.

The blockhouse of the ice-making facility clattered and roared, loud trucks coming and going. From a higher window in one of the

59

fish plants, though, a pretty faced woman smiled at me, and as I left, several more women in another open blockhouse smiled at me as well. They sat at long tables, repairing fishing nets.

Most of them were pregnant.

I left the innocuous scene and its every day toil behind me. An appetite had built up since my ice cream with Mary, and suddenly I was so looking forward to my luncheon with her on the morrow. Nor had I forgotten my dinner appointment with the high-spirited Mr. William Garret, though I regretted I had gleaned no news of his misplaced associate. When a distant bell tolled three times, I knew I'd never last another four hours till dinner so, next, I found myself strolling north up the main road, exiting the town proper.

By now the day's heat got to me. I placed my suit jacket and tie in the briefcase, then continued along. Like Lovecraft, I was accustomed to walking considerable distances daily. *Perhaps the Master strolled this same road as well,* I pondered. Trees lined both sides of the lane. The scenery's tranquility was much welcome after the unpleasant affair with Cyrus Zalen.

Ah! I thought, noticing the mailbox at the end of a long dirt drive on the westward side of the road. The name on the box was Simpson, and all at once, I was tempted to follow Zalen's queer advice and go and introduce myself to Mary's stepfather and children, but then thought better of it. Mary had implied that her stepfather wasn't well. *Better to wait,* came my sensible decision. If destiny would have me meet her stepfather, Mary should be present.

Perhaps the sudden seclusion created the notion, but as I continued along, I received the most aggravating—and most proverbial—impression that I was being watched. Through the woods on the shoreward side I could see quite deeply; I could even see the edges of Innswich Point, but easterly? The woods loomed deep and dark. Just at the fringes of my aural senses I could *swear* I heard something moving, enshrouded. Just a raccoon, more than likely, or simply nothing more than imagination, but immediately the most appetizing aroma came to my nostrils. The roadside stand and smokehouse was just ahead, and now the ragtag sign beckoned me: ONDERDONK & SON. SMOKEHOUSE – FISH-FED PORK. Large penned pigs–five of them–chortled as a youth in his early teens filled their trough with boiled smelts and other bait fish. I was happy to see several bicycles and two motor-cars parked on the roadside, their owners standing in line at the stand. It was always good to witness a prospering enterprise.

When my turn came in line, I was attended by a weathered, overall'd man wearing a crushed train-worker's hat, whom I presumed to be the business' namesake. "What'll be, stranger?" came a gravel-voice inquiry tinted with European accent.

I saw no menu board. "It all smells so wonderful. What items do you offer, sir?"

"Pulled-pork sam-itches, or hocks with greens. What most folks git're the pulled pork. Best yuh've ever et, and if it ain't, it's free."

"A worthy confidence!" I delighted. "Let me have one," and within a moment I was handed a sandwich heaped with said barbeque and half-wrapped in newspaper.

"Take a bite 'fore ya pay," Onderdonk reminded. "Then tell me it ain't the best yuh've ever et."

One bite verified the guarantee. "It's *pre-eminent,* sir," I told him. "I've sampled pulled pork from Kansas City to the Carolinas, and even in Texas, and . . . *this* is superior."

Onderdonk nodded, unimpressed. "'S'what a fishman's gotta do when he can't fish proper. I think the word is *ingenuity.* It was me who thought'a feedin' the swine fish. Makes the meat moister, so's you can smoke it slower and longer."

"It's certainly a recipe for success," I complimented. I insisted he keep the change from my dollar for the twenty-five cent sandwich. "But . . . you're formerly a fisherman?"

"Like my daddy'n his daddy, and so on." The roughened man suddenly soured. "Can't get no fish no more. Ain't right. But this works just fine."

My curiosity was fueled. "You can tell, sir, I'm not from these parts, but what I've noticed in Olmstead–the Innswich Point area–is that fish seem to be more than abundant."

"Sure, it is–for Olmsteaders, which me'n my boy *ain't*, even though we've owned this bit of land since way back." The topic had clearly struck a bad chord. "We'se outsiders far as they're concerned. Anytime me'n my boy been out for a proper day's fishin', they run us off. Rough bunch, some'a them Olmstead fellas. Can't have my boy gettin' beat up over fish."

Territorialism, I knew at once. It was more widespread than most knew; in my own town, lobstering families were known to feud, and clammers, too. "It's regrettable, sir. But the proof of your *ingenuity* has created an alternate market that I'm sure will prosper."

"Mmm," he uttered.

"So I take it this matter of territory forces you to buy the fish with which you feed your pigs."

"Naw, that we can catch ourselfs–see, every night me'n the boy sneak out to the north end'a the Point, throw a few cast nets, then sneak back right after. We ain't more'n ten minutes on the water, then we're gone. It's only enough time to pull up a bucket or two'a bait fish, but that's all we need for the swine."

"Well, at least your system is working," I offered.

"Yeah, I s'pose it is." The man's young son, at this point, came to stand by his father. Onderdonk patted his shoulder. "He works hard for a little shaver, and I want him to learn right. It's the American way."

"Indeed, it is," I said and smiled at the boy, but then to Onderdonk I asked, "I happen to be quite given to pork *ribs* as well. Are they ever on your menu?"

"Ribs? Aw, yeah, but we only do 'em twice weekly. They sell out in a couple'a hours. You come back two days from now, and we'll have some up." He gestured the pig pen. "Soon the boy'n me'll be puttin' Harding in the smoker. Harding's that fat 'un there."

I presumed me meant the largest of the pigs. But I had to laugh. "But you haven't named your *pig* after America's 29ᵗʰ president!"

"That I did!" the working man exclaimed. "And am damn proud of it. 'S was Harding's lollygaggin' and that Tea Pot Dome business that done led to the stock market crashin' and leavin' all of America the way it is!"

Of this I could hardly argue but was still amused.

"Took an *honest* fella–Calvin Coolidge–to give respect back to the nation's highest office, yes sir!" He winked. "Ya won't see none'a my swine named Coolidge, now. But in that sty we also got Taft, Wilson, Garner, and that socialist FDR!"

My. The man certainly had political convictions, odd for a rough-handed working man. "So," I jested. "I'll return day after tomorrow to sample some of *Harding's* smoked ribs!"

"You do that, sir, and ya *won't* be disappointed!"

I bade my farewell, then patted the silent boy on the head and gave him a dollar bill. "A gratuity for you, young man, for doing such good, hard work for your fine father."

"Thank you, sir," the boy peeped.

"A good day to ya!" Onderdonk reveled, and then I walked off.

It did my spirits good to see the working class persevere even in the low economic times. The man was to be admired. Being unfairly barred from the plentitude of local fishing, he'd contravened the obstacle, to succeed nonetheless.

Back down the road I strolled, a mixture of thought now elevating my mood. Certainly, the fine meal, and the equally fine day; the knowledge that tomorrow I would own a rare photograph of H.P. Lovecraft; the likelihood of another fine meal tonight at Wraxall's Eatery, (for, fresh seafood–even more so than pork–was an appreciated indulgence) and just the simple gratification that I was, indeed, walking where Lovecraft once walked.

And there was one other thing, too, which founded my elation.

Mary.

Mary Simpson, I mused. So beautiful. So kind and genuine and hard-working. A uniqueness, even if she *had* once suffered degradations in her unfortunate past. Pregnant with no present husband, still she worked to fulfill her responsibilities. I admitted only now that I was falling in platonic love with her, and platonic it would have to remain for I could not fathom anything more, no matter how urgently I may have wished it.

And I would see her tomorrow for luncheon.

I spun, my heart bucking in my chest. The surprise had taken me with the most unpleasant manner of suddenness.

From the westerly woods I had, for sure, heard a noise.

I was not at all suited for imbroglio, but–now–I knew I was being spied upon, and I was determined not to be harassed.

I peered intensely into the wood, then may have heard a twig snap. "I hear you!" I exclaimed, and did not hesitate to step through the curtain of trees. "Show yourself like a man!"

Several more twigs snapped as my stalker had clearly embarked deeper into the trees. I wasn't sure why, but I continued to give well-gauged chase.

Fifty yards into the woods, a dappling of sunlight betrayed the stalking entity.

For only the briefest second, I glimpsed the figure, not his face but his attire: the long, greasy black raincoat and hood.

"Really, Mr. Zalen, this is no way to treat a paying customer!" my voice surged into the trees. "If it's thievery on your mind, I can assure you, I'm well-armed!"

This much was true, and from my trouser pocket I'd already withdrawn the small hammerless semi-automatic I'd bought at the Colt Patent Firearms Company in Hartford. It was a Model 1903, which I'd read had been the weapon notorious bank robber John Dillinger had carried the day he'd been gunned down. I was not a crack shot, but with a full magazine, I was crack enough.

Zalen stood still but had clearly heard me. At once, he bolted and let himself be swallowed by the woods.

"I'm disappointed, Mr. Zalen!" came my next call. "But, thief or not, don't forget our appointment tomorrow!"

The density of trees soaked up my voice. A shy, retiring sort as myself might be shaken by such a near-confrontation but I felt nothing of the sort. I felt calm, confident, and unwavered, and I had no intention of avoiding Zalen tomorrow. He had something I wanted, and I would pay for it as planned. Now that he'd been apprised that I armed myself, he'd be uninclined for any untoward behavior.

When I turned to reverse myself from the woods and regain the road, I saw the house.

Mary's house, to be sure.

Only the dimmest sunlight penetrated the intricate umbrella of high boughs. The region's all-pervading lack of rainfall had reduced the forest ground to a carpet of tinder. I first dismissed what I was seeing as a hillock, but then a more concentrated scrutiny showed me small, single-paned windows amid a long, vast sprawl of ivy. Eventually I detected corners that had not so been overrun, as well as a slate roof and chimney made of the old tabby bricks from the pre-Revolution period. Beyond the squat and ivy-covered abode, though, stood a clearing radiant with sun and there a lone, wee figure seemed to frolic. As I peered closer, I saw that it was a young boy firing arrows with a crude and more than likely hand-made bow. The arrows were those made for children, with rubber suction cups at their tips, and with these the lad determinedly took aim at an old, propped up window frame which still contained glass.

So this was one of Mary's older children. Odd, though, that only one would be enjoying these splendid outdoors. This close to the house, I expected to hear and see evidence off all eight of her children. *She implied that her stepfather looked after the younger ones,* I recalled. Yet the house sat in an almost palpable silence.

At once, I felt encroaching, even trespassing. It was only the pursuit of Zalen that had led me this deeply into the parched woods. Nevertheless, however impelled to leave, I remained, staring at the leaf-enshrouded house. The impulse to look in a window was very strong, but then I had to chide myself. Not only would that've been the act of a cad–which I was not–it would've been illegal. *I have no right to be here, so I must leave.* But I had to wonder about the motives of my deepest subconscious–or what Freud called the Id.

Was it Mary that my Id hoped to spy upon?

When I turned to leave, I almost shouted.

There, standing immediately before me, was the boy.

I recovered quickly from the start. "Why, hello there, young man. My name is Foster Morley."

"Hello," he replied blushfully. He was thin, bright-eyed, and had that look of so many children: curious wonder and ripe innocence. He looked tenish–it was so hard to tell with adolescents–and had been dressed neatly but in threadbare clothes. One hand held the makeshift bow, the other a quiver of the suction-cupped arrows. After a moment, he said, "My name's Walter, sir."

"Walter, it's a pleasure to meet you." He timidly shook my offered hand. "Now, would your last name happen to be Simpson?"

He seemed to quell surprise. "Yes, sir."

"Well, how do you like that! I'm a friend of your mother's. I spoke to her just this morning at Mr. Baxter's. You should be proud to have such a hard-working mother."

He seemed quietly astonished by this information. "Yes, sir, I'm very proud, and so is my gramps."

His "gramps" could only be Mary's stepfather.

"He's asleep now," he went on. "He's . . . old."

"Yes, and for the elderly we must always have respect." I glanced at his twine-and-tree-switch bow. "My, Walter, you're quite the archer. Practice makes perfect," and then I pointed to his window-frame target from which several arrows had attached themselves, "and by the looks of your impressive skills, you may one day find yourself on the Olympic archery team."

"Do you really think so?" he asked with excitement.

"Of course, if you remain diligent and continue to practice. When you're older, you'll need to train with a real bow, but I'm sure a careful boy such as yourself needn't have to wait much longer for that."

"My mom said I could have a real bow when she makes enough money to buy one. But I can only use it when she's watching."

"That's good advice, son. 'Honor thy mother,' like it says in the Bible."

"Are you here . . . to see her?" he asked. "She's still at work."

I didn't want to lie to the youth, yet I couldn't very well tell him I was pursuing a stalker nearby. "No, Walter, I was merely having a nature walk when I happened upon you and your house. These woods are quite a treat for me, for I spend most of my time in the city. In Providence."

"Oh. I walk in the woods a lot too, sir." He pointed just behind the house. "There's a neat trail right over there that goes all the way back to town through the trees. That's how my mom walks to work every day."

"Why, I'm grateful for your advice, young man," I enthused. "I'll be sure to take that trail back myself. But, tell me. Why are you out here all by yourself? Surely you have brothers and sisters old enough to play with."

His eyes blankened, as though the question were a stifling one. "I have to go now, sir, to help my gramps."

"Of course, and what a fine young man you are to be so attentive to your grandfather." It was all I could say, for it seemed that to press him about my previous question would only put him on the spot. Still, I had to think, *Mary's got seven more children. Are they all in the house?* "But before you're off, Walter, let me give you a present." I was probably out of bounds by doing this, yet I couldn't resist. "And I'm sure your mother and gramps have quite wisely advised you not to take gifts from strangers, but we're not strangers, you and I, are we?"

"No, not really, Mr. Foster," though the mention of a present had clearly throttled his attention.

"What I'd like you to do is take this and buy yourself a better bow," and then I gave him a ten-dollar bill. "And with what's left, wouldn't it be nice to buy your mother some flowers?"

"Oh, yes, sir, it would!" he almost shouted with glee.

"And when your mother asks where you got the money, just say her friend, Mr. Morley."

"Thank you, sir! Thank you a lot!"

"You're quite welcome, Walter. I hope to see you again."

I smiled as he scampered off to the squat house, entered a barely seen door, and disappeared.

What harm could there be? I only hoped I'd made the lad's day. I set to locate Walter's path just behind the house, but again found myself thwarted . . . as more questions occurred. Where exactly *were* the other children? And why had Walter been so reluctant to answer my inquiry?

I skirted round the back of the house, toward the clearing, yet while doing so I deliberately kept an eye out for windows. The last window that would be available to me before I made the clearing was almost entirely ivy-covered.

What could I possibly say for myself should the stepfather see me peering in?

Yet peer in I did, unmindful of the very awkward risk, and why I did this, I'll never be sure.

I only know that I wish I hadn't.

Through the bleary fragment of available glass I first spied a close, brick-lined middle room surrounding a modest fireplace, an additional woodstove, and furniture that I must describe as makeshift. If anything I was glad that they'd improved the utility of their poverty by reusing items–such as boxes, crates, and unattached bricks–for alternate purposes. Several crates, for instance, formed the foundation for a bed and, evidently, a great sack of burlap, stuffed with dried leaves, sufficed for the mattress, over which typical sheets had been lain. A cupboard housed not drinking glasses but reused tin cans for the same purpose. A table, whose top was fashioned by wooded wall slats of irregular length, had legs actually made from stouter tree branches. This glaring squalor injured me...and in my mind I was already calculating how much my wealth would be able to help this destitute but fully functioning family.

I ducked back, when in the moment previous, a door within had opened. Young Walter first appeared, and what followed at his side was a faltering figure and a tap-tap-tapping sound. It was only the sparest daylight through the minute windows that afforded any light at all. The figure, as I squinted, seemed to be using crutches, and though it was through a wedge of darkness that this figure walked, my detection of long, grey hair told me that this could only be Mary's stepfather; Walter was helping him along, toward the makeshift bed.

The oddest noises of protestation resounded when he finally got to the bed and, with great difficulty, managed to lie down in it. I could make out almost nothing in the way of details, but the broader scope of his afflictions–some massive form of arthritis, I presumed–were quite clear by the crookedness of his limbs. Was the hand that picked up the piece of cardboard to use as a fan . . . missing fingers?

"Here's some water, gramps," Walter said and brought him one of the tin cans. My angle showed me little, only Walter carefully tilting the can for him to drink out of. The over-loud chugging sound caused my brow to rise.

"Um, gramps," Walter began. "There was this man, outside. He's a friend of mom's and his name is Foster Morley . . ."

The horrendously palsied figure seemed to lean up, and in doing so I saw a tragically unnatural curve to his spine. But it was Walter's words that had caused him to lean closer.

"And-and . . . he gave me this," the youth hesitated, then showed the ten-dollar bill. "To buy mom some flowers."

The stepfather's reaction to this information is something I'm sure I will never forget.

He lurched forward, deepening the arch to his back, shot out a hand that clearly was deformed, and then emitted a vocal objection in no language I'd ever heard: a high, almost bearing-like squeal underlain with suboctave grunts and what I can only call a mad tweaking, rising and lowering, and an accommodating sound that reminded me of something wet spattering somewhere.

The suddenness–and *unearthliness*–of the man's vociferous objection affected me almost physically, akin to a ball bat across the chest. I lurched backward, yet my eyes remained on that partial window-view and all I can say about what I *think* I saw is this:

Something *shot* forward from the haggard mass of shadows that comprised this infirm man. What that *something* was I cannot accurately delimitate. It was either a length of rope, or a whip, flung forward with a clearly stated maliciousness toward the boy. That's all I can say: it reminded me of a *whip.*

This whip, then, snapped out with a moist but resolute *crack!* and seemed to take the ten-dollar bill from Walter's hand, then draw it back to the afflicted oldster.

An attendant gush of a mix of those dreadfully low suboctaves, and the squeal, and then that awful phlegmatic splatter followed this action, after which the boy, paling before my eyes, turned and dashed from the room.

A tremendous malady, indeed, had accursed this poor elderly man, not just in body but also in mind.

I could witness it no longer, and then I fled myself to the clearing behind the house, fairly bursting into sunlight and a flurry of butterflies, and ran outright until–half-crazed–I spotted the nature trail the boy had apprised me of.

Of congenital defects and progressive disease mechanisms I knew precious little, and though my sense of pity and empathy was sound, I had to forcibly banish the image of this demented and inauspicious man from my mind . . .

As I tramped down the lad's path, I was scarcely aware of its features for several minutes. My heart seemed to hammer in the aftermath of my witness, and my breath grew short. Eventually I slowed to regain my senses, then stooped, hands on knees, to rest.

The rapid exodus from the maledict house left me in a dirt-scratch of a trail lined by man-tall grasses. Insects chirruped and the sun blazed.

It was the darkness of the huddled house, I thought, *and the potency of suggestion that so grotesquely appended what I saw.*

Of all people, I thought again of Cyrus Zalen and his all-too-true implications regarding my status in life. *A rich pud.* My unearned station of privilege had shielded me from such tragic realities heaped upon the less fortunate, and this, simply, wasn't right. I needed to *know* these direful realities–*and* their consequences–to be the better man that I'm sure God wanted me to be. My empathy must not be staged, nor my pity manufactured. I fancied myself a philanthropist–a willful *contributor* to those who had sorely less than me.

I knew that I must contribute *more*, and more, too, than simply money.

Soft voices severed my thoughts. When I turned my head, a great glimmer flashed in my eyes; through the tall grass, I saw a modest lake full of floating sunlight. But the voices...

It was necessary to shield my eyes to annul the glare. There, sitting at a short pier's end, were two women, one honey-blond and the other obsidian-haired. Both were naked, chatting animatedly as they rowed their feet in the water. I saw a small bottle serving as a buoy farther out in the lake.

The girls' bare white backs gleamed in the sun, but the tranquil scene did not parallel the apparent mood of the coal-haired one, who snapped, "I just *hate* it, Cassandra! It sickens me–their condition, I mean. And I have to go again tonight. Oh, God, I dread it *so much.*"

71

"So you're not in the way yet?" queried the other.

"No, I don't think so. They make me go–every night–until they're sure." The girl seemed to hack. "And I have to be with several of them! One's not enough! It's got to be at least two each night, and I heard they've gotten two more. What's that now, seven all together?"

"Six, I think. Remember, the one died, and that curly-haired man couldn't . . . you know. You never know when one might not be any good all of a sudden. Sometimes they wind up like Paul."

Paul! the name immediately struck me. A common name, yes, but could they be referring to Mary's invalid brother?

"Well, shit!" exclaimed the black-haired waif with a surprising profanity. "One per night should be enough!"

"It's like the doctor said, Monica. The more you do it with, the better chance of success . . ."

What on earth are they talking about? I wondered, puzzled. And . . . the *doctor?* Did they mean Dr. *Anstruther?*

"That's why he tests them every so often," the honey-blonde continued. "To make sure they haven't lost their . . . I forgot the word. Portense? Er–no, potency!"

I stared at these strange words, my face lengthening.

"But they're just so *ugly* like that!" the dark-haired one, Monica, nearly squealed in objection. "It gives me nightmares."

The honey-blonde, Cassandra, took Monica's hand to offer a consolation. "It's like they say, you've got to get the right frame of mind. It's not about pleasure, it's about something much more important. To think like you're thinking is to be selfish. And they *have* to be the way they are–for safety's sake . . ."

"Ugh! It's just *awful* . . ."

"You don't have to tell me, Monica. I've had six babies so far. It's just the way it is here. It's better for the future."

"I don't know how you could've done it *six times!*"

Cassandra answered dreamily. "You just close your eyes and think *nice* things, Monica. You pretend you're with someone else, someone handsome and strong and sweet and–"

"Someone normal!" Monica upheld her complaints. "Not all girls do it *their* way."

"No, but their way keeps us in their favor, like the doctor says."

Monica seemed to be near tears. "God, why can't I have a real man just once? Sometimes I'm tempted to leave."

"Shh! Don't talk like that!" chided Cassandra. "We both know what happens to girls who try to leave . . ."

I couldn't have been more bewildered as I listened to the arcane discourse . . .

"I better check the trap," said Cassandra, and she hopped down into chest-deep water. She was wading out toward the makeshift buoy. Meanwhile, Monica stood up to stretch, hands behind her back. She did so turning, which afforded me a side-glance of her physique. She bore a stunning, willowy beauty in her youth, and couldn't have been more than eighteen. Next she turned more, and was facing me as she continued to stretch. The shining black hair rose in a brief breeze off the water. She was an exotic sight, petite-breasted, long-legged, and flat-stomached. I meant to turn away, for my inadvertent glimpse of her seemed invasive, but then Cassandra returned. She climbed up the pier's ladder to the deck, hoisting with her a small wire trap filled with crayfish. Unlike Monica, Cassandra was nine months pregnant if she was a day.

"Look, it's full!" she enthused over the trap full of skittering things.

Monica came over. "Wow, that is a lot." She tested the trap's weight. "It must be ten pounds! We'll have chowder for *days!*"

As I listened further, my closer attentions lapsed . . . and my hand slipped. I dropped my briefcase . . .

The sound was all too obvious; both girls snapped their inquisitive gazes in my direction. Could they see me? I didn't move a muscle.

"I think someone's there," Cassandra suspected, then she brought a fretful finger to her lips. "God, I hope it's not *them* . . ."

"Look! There!" Monica pointed directly at the stand of grass I hid behind.

"Is it . . ."

"No, it's a man! A *real man!*" She strode naked off the pier. "Hey, wait! Come here!"

I grabbed my case, and slipped out.

"No!" wailed Monica. "Don't go! *Please!* We can make you real happy! COME BACK!"

I had no intention of complying. My feet took me swiftly down the close path, and I could only hope that neither girl had seen enough of my face to recognize it later. In the distance, I heard Monica's final grievance. "Oh, SHIT! He ran away!"

My pace did not abate until I was back at the Town Center and gratefully entering the Hilman House . . .

Secure in my room, I sat on the bed to regain my breath. I turned the RCA on, for music would remind me of normalcy, and I immediately relaxed to "Our Love," by Tommy Dorsey. But this would be followed by the hourly news broadcast: a labor strike is ruled illegal by the Supreme Court, General Francisco Franco conquers Madrid with his fascist troops, a scientist named Fermi warns allied governments that a process now exists which can split atoms and thus harness a terrible destructive force. None of this news sounded hopeful; I switched it off.

The distraction I hoped for was sabotaged. *What exactly HAPPENED today?* I queried myself in some disillusionment. I tried with diligence to find a common logic in what I'd seen and heard but in the end failed. I could make no sense of it, but I considered that in my current expended and excited state, it would do me good to calm down to resort my thoughts. The day's heat as well as the mad sprint had left me grimy and saturated with perspiration, so I had a cool bath in the private tub. I tried to clear my thoughts . . .

But a sudden fatigue left me drowsy even in the cool water. I drifted in and out of a half-sleep. Snippets of dreams harassed me: images of not only perplexity but also repugnance.

The man in the squalid house, deformed by some catastrophic arthritic symptom, unleashing wet, gushing invectives in no way intelligible, and then lashing at young Walter with that whip, or whatever it might have been.

And the two nude girls on the pier, one pregnant and then one evidently fearing pregnancy with an appalled resignation . . . Their cryptic words slipped in and out of my half-dreaming mind:

–it sickens me–their condition, I mean–

–so you're not in the way yet?–

–they make me go–every night–until they're sure!–

–sometimes they wind up like Paul . . . –

The words blended, then, with a razor-crisp recollection of their physical bodies, their gleaming nude beauty, their shimmering white skin, and their private feminine features so forbidden–and so wrong for me to have willingly looked upon–yet so exotic . . .

I may have slipped into a deep doze when these vivid images were singularly banished . . . by the image of Mary . . .

First, the loveliness of her face and simple honest manner, and even some of her remarks:

–a handsome, well-mannered gentleman like you? Never married?–

And then a devilish meld: my first captivating image of her working at Baxter's slowly contorting itself into the image on the nefarious and wholly exploitative photograph I'd bought from the despicable Cyrus Zalen: Mary, laid out bare and pregnant and thrust-bosomed as the visual photographic fodder of degenerates . . .

The finality of that image shocked me from my doze, and I'm sure I audibly groaned. The sudden anxiety was one–I'm ashamed to say–of unquenched physical desire of the most sinful sort. It left me carnally evoked, and though in the past I'd always done better than a fair job of abstaining, the primal necessity, now, could not be extinguished. I need not go on in detail save to say that my frenzy forced me to do what solitary men are *known* to do in such moments of weakness, after which–steeped in shame–I prayed God's forgiveness for this venal and most insolent offense to His grace . . .

Embarrassed after the fact, I languished in the claw-footed tub, but then my eyes shot wide–

I'd heard, with some distinction, a sudden and undeniable sound: the desperate hitching of a single breath into one's chest. It was a lush, wanton sound, more than likely female.

I stared at the opposing wall to at once be inundated by the notion that I was being observed remotely. But if so . . .

From where exactly?

I jumped from the bath, donned a robe, and, like a paranoiac, actually began to examine the opposing wall and the ceiling over the tub. But no "peepholes" were chanced upon; minutes later, I frowned at myself for the foolish overreaction. The sound I thought I'd heard was most certainly a remnant from the dream-fragments and a fatigued body and mind. *For goodness sake!* I mocked. *Who would be spying on me, of all people?*

My new Pierce Chronograph wristwatch showed me my dinner appointment was fast approaching. I talced myself, brushed my teeth with a new product called Listerine Tooth-Cleaning Paste, then dressed in my evening suit. Though I was looking forward to dining with Mr. Garret, most of my thoughts focused on a different appointment: my luncheon date with Mary tomorrow. I oddly felt that I'd sullied her by my previous act of debasement and self-abusiveness, an absurd abstraction, but such was me. Nevertheless, I would not leave until I'd done one simple thing.

I sat at the small writing table the room provided, and opened my briefcase. From it I withdrew the folder I'd purchased from Zalen, and from the bottom of the assortment of old photos within, I slipped out the shot of Mary. It was with a plummeting grimness that

I allowed myself to look at it . . .

The photo's sharpness, contrast, and overall clarity seemed even more precise than before, and again I was stifled by the sense of fusion that joined Mary's objective physical beauty with a revoltingly exploitative design: that graceful and exuberant pose, all for the visual consumption of unholy men given to perversity. Every element of the photograph seemed to beckon me to lust–Mary's bottomless, sparkling eyes; her sighing smile; the high, dark-nippled breasts burgeoning with milk; the toned, shapely legs. I noticed now that every inch of her impeccable nudity either shined in profuse sweat or had been deliberately glazed by some kind of oil, the effect of which caused the entirety of her image to shimmer as if alive within the borders of the photographic paper. But I would not succumb to the lust that this image tried to seduce.

Only love.

A monstrous world, to allow this, I resolved. *To enslave the poor and the desperate for the most jaded of intents.* I took up a small pair of folding shears from my travel kit and began to shred the photo, from the borders in, until all that was left was the tiny square of Mary's beauteous visage. The shreddings I discarded; the square, however, I hid in a pocket of my wallet.

Down the stairwell, then, I went; as I neared the entry level, though, the door to the atrium opened before I could reach it, and suddenly I was faced by a slim, attractive young woman in a nice but simple frock gown that so many preferred in the warmer months; she was on her way up as I was on my way down. She lent me a meek smile, then nodded as we converged.

"How do you do?"

"Hello," was all she said as if shy. When she passed me, I was stung by a tremulous shock; it had taken me this long for the girl's willowy figure and obsidian-black hair to register.

Monica, I felt sure. *One of the pier girls . . .*

She'd obviously not recognized me as the interloper she'd been so ardently pleading with just a few hours ago.

Certainly she's not staying here . . . Perhaps she was employed here with the housekeeping service. But, really, why should I be concerned?

I heard her quiet footfalls as she mounted the steps, then passed myself into the atrium, but as the door was closing behind me–and I'm not sure why I noticed this but–the aforesaid footfalls seemed to terminate very quickly. Nor was I sure what compelled me to my next gesture . . .

I went back into the stairwell and looked upward.

No evidence of Monica could be discerned, but then–

click!

The sound registered quickly enough to bid me to glance up at the door on the second-floor landing. It clicked shut before my eyes.

The second floor, I thought. *The LOCKED floor.* Monica, for whatever reason, clearly had access to it.

My frown returned me to the atrium. Why this addled me I couldn't guess . . .

The congenial bellhop and desk clerk greeted me as I passed. Of the clerk, I had to inquire: "If you don't mind, sir, I'm curious as to the reason for the second floor being locked."

It may have been imaginativeness on my part, but his standard smile and good nature seemed to snap off for a moment. "But, you're on the *fourth* floor, Mr. Morley. Why would you . . ."

"Of course!" I tried to sound dismissive. "I should've preambled that I just now mistakenly took the second floor for the first." I would not quite call this a lie but, say, a modest divergency from the truth.

But the man's good-natured expression had already restored itself. "Ah, well, the floor's being kept locked for the time being. Renovations. The work shouldn't take more than a month."

"I see. Well, thank you, good man, for satisfying my fairly useless curiosity. I should've guessed!" and then I bid him a good evening.

Across the street, then, to Wraxall's Eatery, where an appetizing aroma awaited. The establishment was spotless, and appointed with simple chairs and tables, plus a none-too-surprising nautical motif: photos of old, rain-slickered waterman proudly displaying sizable fishes, a ship's wheel and a ship's glass, fishing nets with floats adorning the corners. I supposed it possible that, before the government renewal, this very eatery may have been the dismal cafeteria in which Robert Olmstead begrudgingly dined as unwholesome loafers cast strange glances.

Brass lanterns quaintly housing candles ornamented each wooden table. My eyes thinned, though, when I noticed that Mr. Garret was nowhere in sight. Only one table was occupied, by a soft-speaking couple.

When the hostess turned, bearing a menu, she was struck speechless.

I couldn't have been more pleased! It was Mary . . .

"Why, Mary, what a pleasant surprise," I tried to contain my joy.

"Foster!" She smiled and pressed a hand to my back to urge me to the corner. "Take the window booth. The view's lovely as the sun sets. I'm so glad you could come."

"I had no idea you worked here as well."

"Oh, I just fill in sometimes. But the money's not bad, now that our wonderful president has signed the Minimum Wage Act."

I'd read of this: a rather scrimy forty-cents per hour. But then I had to keep reminding myself that chance–and my father's hard work, not my own–had handed me a status much more fortunate than that of most.

She filled my water glass as I took a seat. "Did you find a nice, quiet place to read your book?"

"Oh, *The Shadow Over Innsmouth* . . ." I'd almost forgotten that had been my original goal. "Actually, I was so busy gallivanting about town that I never got round to it. Tomorrow, though. After our lunch date, which I dearly hope is still on."

Suddenly she sighed, then drooped her head dramatically. "Are you kidding? I can't wait. It'll be my first afternoon off in weeks."

This disconcerted me. "Mary, there's nothing more admirable than a hard-worker," and then I leaned close, "but I wish you didn't have to put in such hours while you're with child."

"You're so sweet, Foster," she grinned and squeezed my hand. "But hard work is what made America, isn't it?"

"Yes, it is," I said, if a bit guiltily.

"Besides, Dr. Anstruther says it's fine to work until the eighth month, just nothing too strenuous."

I'm sure this were true, but it still bothered me. When she leaned over to hand me the menu, I could detect a bit of her bosom's valley, then recalled, first, the jaded photograph and, next, the split-second glimpse I'd caught of her breast in the back room of Baxter's. Then there it was again, that perfect valley of flesh.

I nearly ground my teeth as I looked away. God! I hope she hadn't noticed . . .

Another distraction was needed, but this time, I needn't manufacture one. A brass ship's clock on the wall showed me I was five minutes late. "Say, Mary? Has a respectably dressed man, perhaps in his late-'20s, been in? Brown, short hair? His name is William Garret."

She shook her head. "No, Foster. Mid-week is always slow—like they say, Friday is Fish Day. There'll be a rush later, when the watermen come back from the docks. But I'm afraid I haven't seen the man you're describing."

"I was supposed to meet him," I began, but then shrugged it off. "No matter. He's either running late, or maybe he secured himself a position. He's an accountant."

"Well, they might need accountants in the wholesalers," she offered.

"Yes, I'm sure that's it." It was obvious. He'd probably located his friend Mr. Poynter and managed to get a job. I truly wished the best for him.

Following some more small talk, I got about my order, which Mary had recommended: chowder, fried Ipswich clams, and striped bass stuffed with rock crab. I'd always delighted in such fare, and felt bad that Lovecraft himself, a New Englander, too, could never share in these delights due to a repugnance for shellfish. My eyes, however, struggled to keep averted from Mary as she went about her table-waiting. *She's just so . . . beautiful,* I kept thinking. Eventually the other table left, then a man from the back exited the restaurant as well, seeming to head down the block. Next thing I knew Mary was sitting across from me, with two Cocamalts.

"I love your company, Mary, but might not your employer–"

"Don't worry about Mr. Wraxall," she excused, and sipped her drink. "Every night at seven he goes to the bar–Karswell's–for at least three boxcars. So I can take a break, too, while your food's cooking."

"How delightful," I all but exclaimed.

Even in her nonchalance, her eyes cast a glitter akin to diamond chips, and I could see the richness of her dark blond hair now that it had been freed from the hairnet she wore in the general store. When I caught myself watching her lips surround the drink-straw, I almost cringed at the sudden eroticism of it.

"So, how was your gallivanting?" she asked.

"Splendid, Mary. I'm sure I toured most of the town proper–"

"The docks?" she cut in.

"Oh, yes, the docks too."

"Don't be put off if the watermen weren't overly friendly," she informed.

"Actually, my friend Mr. Garret warned me of it, but in truth I scarcely noticed any such workmen."

"It's only because they're . . . what's the word?" A fingertip went to her mouth. "Possessive."

This seemed curious. "Possessive? Whatever do you mean?"

"They don't like strangers, Foster," she went on. "Strangers shouldn't be in our harbor, they should stay in their own. We don't send our boats to Rockport or Gloucester. Why should they be allowed to send theirs here?"

Now it made sense; this was the territorialism of which the man Onderdonk spoke of so bitterly. A "stranger" from another port town could easily take note of where the Innswich fishing boats were casting their nets, as well as their time tables. "It seems a fair rule of thumb," I said, "and I'm happy that the town's fishing industry is doing so well." I reflected on a pause. "I only hope that *you're* doing well, too, Mary."

"Oh, me? I'm fine. I'm making more right off the bat with the new minimum wage, and since I turned twenty-five, I've been receiving a monthly dividend from the town collective."

"The town . . . collective?" I chuckled half-heartedly. "It sounds a bit socialist."

"No, it's just a profit-sharing plan for residents who work and contribute to the local economy," she explained. "Most of it comes from the fishing. I've been getting it three years now, and each year it goes up a little." She lowered her voice. "I'm ashamed to say, but we don't even have any real furniture at our house, but this year, thanks to the collective, I'll be able to buy some."

The remark sunk my heart; I recalled from my brief visit to her house the makeshift oddments that Mary's poverty forced her to use as furniture. "You're a determined woman, Mary, and with all those children? Plus your brother and stepfather to care for? Your resilience is quite remarkable. I must confess, though, I actually met your son Walter today. What a fine lad."

This admission seemed to hold her in check. "You've . . . been to my house?"

I had to choose my phrases carefully. "Not really. I was simply walking by, returning from the barbeque stand up the road."

Her words faltered. "And . . . you met . . . Walter?"

"Indeed, I did. What an industrious young man. He was practicing–quite deftly–his archery skills. I'd only a moment to speak with him, though."

"But you didn't . . . see my . . . stepfather?"

"Oh, no, no. I was just passing by," I reiterated. "I like Walter very much, but, I'll tell you, I didn't see hide'nor hair of your other children. You've a total of eight, right?"

"Yes, but they're younger. They were probably napping."

"No doubt, on such a hot day." The temptation dragged at me: to simply write her a cheque for $5000 and give it to her, for a *new* house, with *real* furniture, to ease her squalor.

But I feared how that might be taken at this point . . .

"And I hope you're not terribly disappointed with me, Mary, but circumstance forced me to break my promise of earlier," I went on. "I did pursue an interview with this Mr. Cyrus Zalen earlier today–"

"Oh, Foster, you didn't!" she exclaimed.

I raised a reassuring finger. "It was of little consequence, really. You see, I simply couldn't deprive your brother of his photograph with H.P. Lovecraft; it didn't seem right. And as good fortune would have it, Zalen is still in possession of the negative, and I've arranged to purchase a copy from him tomorrow. But you were quite right about one thing," I said with a chuckle. "He's one of a shady lot indeed."

Mary's sudden downcast expression instantly made me regret volunteering this information. But I plainly didn't like the idea of keeping it from her.

"He's a bad man, Foster," she implored. "And it's a filthy area he lives in. He's a drug addict and a con man."

"I've no doubt, now that I've met him."

"And he preys on people–on *women,* Foster. Poor women."

"I can imagine," I said.

Now she gulped. "And I'm sure . . . he told you about me."

Here I had no choice but to lie, to spare her feelings. "Why do you say that? He had nothing at all to say of you."

She reached across and touched my hand again. "Foster, I have to be honest with you–because I *like* you so much–"

The sudden comment rocked me . . .

"–but a long time ago I was one of the women he preyed upon," she finished and then looked right at me.

There was no hesitation in my response, nor with my smile. "Mary, there are times when we *all* take an erroneous path in life, and when we do unethical deeds out of desperation, we're only being human. These are not grievous sins, and what you must believe is that God forgives all."

Her eyes were a blink away from tearing up. "Does He really?"

"Yes," I assured her, and now it was my hand that took hers. "The entails of motherhood are burdensome indeed. The past is behind you now, and any of your past misgivings are behind you as well. The same goes for all of us, Mary. The same goes for me. You're doing the right thing now, and you have a wonderful future that awaits you."

She was choking up, squeezing my hand. "I'll just have out with it then, because I can't lie to you," and then she croaked, "before the town collective admitted me, there were times, in the past, when I'd had to resort to acts of prostitution."

"But that doesn't *matter*," I replied, unfazed–for this I already knew. "You're a moral, honest, and very hardworking woman now. *That's* all that matters, Mary."

She looked at me so strangely then. "I can tell by your eyes–it really doesn't bother you, does it–I mean, what I was in the past."

"It bothers me not in the least," I told her with all my heart. "I'm only interested in what you are now: a wonderful, beautiful person."

She hitched on a few sobs as a bell rang, and someone yelled "Order up!"

She wiped her eyes, smiling. "Foster, the first time in years I've felt good about myself is right *now*–thanks to you."

"You have every reason to feel good about yourself, and I hope you *always* do."

"I better get your dinner before I start on a full-blown bawling spell," and then she was up and rushing into the back.

I sat, now, in a platonic ecstasy. This lovely woman seemed to be genuinely fond of me, something rare in my life of indulgent seclusion. What made me happiest was knowing that my words and earnestness had helped give her a more positive conception of herself.

When my dinner was brought, it was an aproned cook and not Mary who'd brought it. "Sorry, sir, but your waitress is indisposed for a moment. All tearing up about something."

"Allergies, I'm sure," I said. "And thus far she's done a marvelous job in attending to me."

"Enjoy your dinner, sir."

"I'm certain I will, thank you."

As I dined on this sumptuous feast, I noted varnished plaques mounted on the walls–they were name-planks for old ships. HETTY, one read, and the others: SUMATRY QUEEN and COLUMBY. I couldn't be sure why–and perhaps it was the diversion of the ambrosial meal, but . . . did those names ring a bell.

The chowder proved superior to the standard Providence recipe, and the striped bass may have been the best I'd ever sampled. Toward the meal's end, I felt like the most sinful of gluttons, especially in times when food was scarce for so many.

Mary returned–freshened up now, and recomposed–and after she cleared the table, she sat down again opposite me. I couldn't have complimented the meal more. But her look told me something still troubled her.

"What you said earlier, Foster," she began, "about Cyrus Zalen? You said you're seeing him *again?*"

"Yes, tomorrow at four." I knew she wasn't comfortable about me being in this cad's proximity, so I meant to assure her. "It's purely to purchase a copy of the Lovecraft photo, so that your brother won't be deprived of his. Zalen needed some time to process the negative.

85

But after that, I give you my guarantee, it will be the last time I ever cross paths with the man."

"That's good, Foster. He has a bad way about him–he's a conniver."

And also the father of one of your children, the darker thought flashed in my head. *But he'll never connive you anymore, Mary. I'll see to it.* "A conniver and then some," I went on, in a more light-hearted voice. "I caught the man actually stalking me twice today, once before I met him and once after."

"Stalking you?"

"Slinking about from the woods, tailing me. I'm sure robbery was what he was considering. I'd walked up to the Onderdonk's stand for a sandwich, and it was on my way back that Zalen began to follow me more overtly. I went in the woods after him, to show him I wasn't afraid of his kind."

"Foster, you shouldn't have!"

"The man knows I have some means, so I guess he figured robbing me might yield more profit than my purchase of the Lovecraft photo. But I made it quite plain to him that I was well-able to defend myself. He'll not be doing that again, I'm sure. But this unpleasant incident occurred not too far from where young Walter was engaged in his archery session–that's how I came to meet him. Zalen was long gone by then." Naturally I neglected to add that it was Zalen who revealed the rough location of Mary's ramshackle house.

"The man's like a blight," she bemoaned. "It's rare that I see much of him but when I do . . . all it does . . . it reminds me–"

I squeezed her hand in reassurance. "You must disregard any negative memories that are triggered by Zalen. He counts for nothing. Revel, instead, in the promise of your future. I assure you, it will be a bright one."

She looked sullenly at me. "Oh, how I wish that were true, Foster."

My only response was a smile, for I'd decided to say no more. It wasn't necessary because at that moment, I already knew what I was going to do . . .

After a bit more small talk, I rose and prepared to excuse myself. "Well, by now it's certain that Mr. Garret won't be making an appearance, and I'm a bit fatigued from a day of travel. But please know, Mary, that spending this little bit of time with you was the highlight of my day. You're a lovely person."

She blushed and blinked another tear away. Then she glanced about to see that no one was looking, and kissed me quickly on the lips. I shivered in a sweet shock.

Her lips came right to my ear. "Please come and see me at the store tomorrow. I'm off at twelve."

"I'll be there. We'll have a fabulous lunch somewhere."

Then she hugged me in something like desperation. "Please, don't forget."

I chuckled. "Mary. No force on earth could make me forget."

Another quick kiss and she pulled away, then picked up the fifty-dollar bill I'd left on the table. "I'll be right back with your change." When she hustled away into the back, I quietly left the restaurant.

The sky was darkening in a spectacular fashion as I made the main street. The sinking sun painted wisps of clouds with impossible light over the waterfront. The street's quaint cobblestones seemed to shine in a glaze; neatly dressed passersby strolled gaily along, the perfect human accouterment to an evening rife with tranquil charm. At that moment, it occurred to me: I'd never felt more content.

It was a shrill siren that ripped the evening's placidity. I turned the corner and noticed a long red and white ambulance pulled right up on the sidewalk, with several uniformed attendants bustling about. Several residents stood aside, looking on with concern.

What's this all about? I thought, then felt my spirit plummet when I noticed that the commotion was centered around the bargain store I'd visited previously. At the same moment a stretcher was borne out from the shop, and on it was a very still and very blanch-faced Mr. Nowry. In the doorway, the man's expectant wife sobbed openly.

Oh, no . . .

"Poor Mr. Nowry," a small voice announced to my side. "He was such a nice man."

I turned to see an attractive red-haired woman standing next to me. "I-I hope he hasn't expired. He was as congenial a man as you could ever hope to meet; why, I spoke to him just hours ago."

"Probably another coronary attack," she ventured.

"I'll go and see," I said, and made my way to the receding commotion. "Sir? I'm sorry to intrude," I asked of one of the ambulance men, "but could you confide in me as to the status of Mr. Nowry?"

The younger man looked bleary-eyed from a long day. "I'm afraid he died a few minutes ago. There was nothing we could do this time–his ticker finally went out."

I bowed my head. "I scarcely knew him, but he was a good man from what I could see."

"Oh, sure, an Olmsteader through and through." He forearmed his brow. "But it's been a strange day, I'll tell ya."

"In what way?"

"Small town like this, we don't get more than two of three deaths a year, but today? We've had *two* now."

"Two? How tragic."

Now the stretcher bearing the decedent was loaded into the rear compartment of the vehicle. The man to whom I was speaking pointed inside. "A young girl, too, not a half-hour ago. One of those not in with a decent crowd, but still . . . She died in childbirth."

I looked to where he was pointing and noticed a second stretcher.

Instantly, my throat thickened.

It was a thin, lank-haired girl in her twenties who lay dead next to Mr. Nowry, a sheet covering her to the chin. Even in the pallor of death, though, I recognized her face.

It was Candace–one of Zalen's ill-reputed photo models and prostitutes. But the great, swollen belly was gone now, only swollen breasts showing beneath the white sheet.

"Please, tell me her baby survived," I implored.

"The baby's fine," he said matter-of-factly.

"Praise God . . ."

The man looked at me in the oddest way, then closed the long back door of the hospital coach, and went on his way.

I returned to the woman I'd been talking to. "I'm afraid Mr. Nowry has passed away. We should be sure to remember him in our prayers." I took a doleful glance to his poor widow, still sobbing in the shop doorway. "I pity his wife, though."

"She's expecting any day now," the woman told me with something hopeful in her tone. "You needn't worry; the Nowrys are long-term town-members. The collective will provide for his widow."

Another reference to this collective. My initial impression had been less than positive due to unavoidable insinuations but now, it seemed, I may have been hasty. The initiative, instead, sounded like a very serviceable system of social/fiscal management and profit-sharing. It was heartening to know that Mrs. Nowry wouldn't be left on her own. As for Candace's newborn . . . well, I could only assume it would be cared for by family members or placed in a fosterage program.

"You're new in town," said the redhead with the most traceable smile. Then she sighed. "Just passing through, I fear."

"Why, yes, but why do you put it that way?"

"The handsome men *never* stay long."

The flattering comment took me off guard. "That's, uh, very nice of you to say, Miss, but I must bid you a good evening now." I walked away quickly. Being complimented so abruptly by women always left me tongue-tied. At least it left me, however selfishly, with a good feeling. I'd certainly never thought of myself as *handsome*. I smiled, then, when I recalled Mary making similar comment.

The desk shift had changed when I was back at the Hilman House; a stoop-shouldered older woman tended the desk.

"Ma'am, I'd like to write a note to one of your guests, a Mr. William Garret," I told her. "Would you be so kind as to pass it on to him?"

A moment of fuddlement crossed her eyes. She glanced at a ledger. "Oh, dear, I'm afraid Mr. Garret checked out several hours ago, along with another associate of his."

"Would that be Mr. Poynter?"

"Why, yes, sir, that's correct. They caught the motor-coach to the transfer station. Headed back to Boston, I believe."

"I see. Well thank you for your time."

That explained that, though I regretted not seeing Garret again, if only to bid him good luck in the future. At least he'd re-found his friend Poynter. It was too bad they hadn't secured positions here.

Back upstairs, I passed a cart-pushing maid in the hall. She smiled and said hello. It took a moment to recognize her.

It was the maid I'd spoken to upon checking in, the pregnant one, though now...

She no longer displayed any signs of gravidness.

"Why, my dear girl!" I exclaimed. "I see you've borne your child . . ."

"Yes, sir," she said rather flatly. "A boy."

"Well, congratulations are in order but–really!–you should be resting, not working!"

She stared at me, head atilt, mulling her thoughts. "I'm just picking up a bit, sir, then I can go home."

"But it's unacceptable for an employer to insist you work so soon after–"

"Really, sir, I appreciate your concern but I'm feeling all right. I'll be to bed very soon."

"I should hope so." This was mortifying. And with all the new labor laws in place to protect against such exploitation. "Where's the baby?"

An odd pause stalled her. "Home, sir. With my mother . . ." She gave a meek smile that struck me as forced, and went on with her cart.

Off all the things, I thought. All the more reason for Mary to be out of here. Town collective or not, workers–most especially *pregnant women*–shouldn't be used as an objective resource. Certain medical conditions must always be given leeway.

I'd already decided that I was going to take Mary and her entire family back to Providence with me. Should it turn out to be a mistake, then so be it. At least I will have tried. My only fret was how and when to make my desires known. It was of the utmost importance that she know nothing was expected of her in return, which might be difficult to convince her of, given the darker aspects of her past.

I will remove her from her burdens, I determined, *and give her the life she deserves. And maybe, just maybe . . .*

One day I'd have the privilege of marrying her.

So much for my "platonic" intents, but it was imperative that I be honest with myself. Of course, my idealism was strong, and I knew that things didn't always germinate into what we truly wanted.

But I knew what *I* wanted. I wanted *her. And I will make every effort to be the man she longs for but has thus far never had.*

I knew that I had to buff not only the edges of my outrage over the young maid's exploitation, but also the sad mishap of Mr. Nowry's coronary attack–I needed to let my mind stray elsewhere. I decided to relax, then, in the clean room's quietude, so I sat up in my bed and opened my most cherished book: *The Shadow Over Innsmouth.* It would not be a concerted re-reading, I'd decided; that would come tomorrow when I found the perfect place, perhaps in view of the harbor. Though the buildings were different, the inlet itself and the mysterious sea beyond was the same that Lovecraft spied when the korms of his masterpiece were first coming to mind, a brilliant amalgamation of atmosphere, concept, character, and, ultimately, horror. Evidently, Lovecraft had been so irrevocably impacted by Irwin Cobb's sophomoric yet deeply macabre "Fishhead," and also Robert Chambers' flawed but image-steeped "The Harbour Master" that he'd seized the basic seeds of these stories and taken them into ingenious new directions, to weave very much his own superior tale of symbolic–and wholly monstrous–miscegenation. In it, when narrator Robert Olmstead accidentally stumbles upon the crumbling and legend-haunted Innsmouth seaport, he discovers, first, that the townsfolks have long-since assumed a pact of sorts with a race of horrid amphibious sea creatures first discovered by one Captain Obed Marsh, a sea-trader, while venturing through the East Indies; and, second and worst, that this monstrous and greed-driven pact involved not only human sacrifice but also the rampant crossbreeding of the creatures–the Deep Ones–and the human populace of Innsmouth. Any page I turned to led to an image or a line that I could easily deem my favorite.

Here was one, a line of dialogue spoken by none other than the "ancient toper" Zadok Allen, whose real-life model had been Zalen's grandfather, Adok. The line read as thus: "Never was nobody like Cap'n Obed–old limb o' Satan! Heh, heh! I kin mind him a-tellin' abaout furren parts, an' callin' all the folks stupid fer goin' to Christian meetin' an' bearin' their burdens meek an' lowly. Say they'd orter git better gods like some o' the folks in the Injies–gods as ud bring 'em good fishin' in return for their sacrifices, an' ud reely answer folks's prayers."

Naturally I was amused by the convenient parallel: the "good fishing" that the Deep Ones brought to Innsmouth in exchange for bloody oblations. I had to chuckle at this very *real* town's own abundance of local fish. I nearly laughed aloud!

Something that I suspect as being subconscious caused my errant page-flipping to stop, and next my eyes were locked down strangely on another line of Zadok Allen's drunken ramble: "Obed Marsh he had three ships afloat–brigantine *Columby,* brig *Hetty,* an' bark *Sumatry Queen...*"

A vertigo accosted me as I stared at the words. Then: *Of course! I knew I'd seen those names before! They were right here all along* . . . , for now I recalled these same names from the decorative ship plaques in the restaurant.

So not only did the town of "Innsmouth" exist, though under its true and none-too-different name Innswich, but so did these trading vessels exist somewhere in the town's dim past. I couldn't help but admire the assiduousness of Lovecraft's research efforts–something he was quite known for–to plumb such minute details of reality and infuse them into his fictional landscape.

I re-read parts of several more scenes, all with much chilling delight, then put the book up with the heated anticipation of re-reading cover to cover tomorrow. But there was one more even greater anticipation regarding tomorrow . . .

I must make every effort to look my best, I realized, then shuddered when I opened my suitcase and found my best suit in a crumpled state. There'd be no place open this hour to get them freshly pressed; hence, I could only hope . . .

When I glanced into the closet, I saw I was in luck! There, leaning, stood a collapsible pressing board, and atop the high shelf sat a steam-iron. I knew next to nothing of such procedures, but how difficult could it be? I took out the pressing board, looking for some sort of locking pin in order to extend its legs, when–

"Drat!"

–it slipped from my fingers and banged against the back wall of the closet.

"Oh, for pity's sake!" I complained aloud when I saw that the meager board had struck the wall with such impact that it actually left a hole. *The management will be none-too-pleased over this,* I thought. *Until I pay them double the repair fee.* I stepped inside to retrieve the board, then lowered to a knee to inspect the damage. Bits of plaster lay about, while the insult to the plaster-board looked a foot long and several inches wide. This was flimsy construction to say the least, yet of the bungling accident I could only blame my own carelessness.

Before I could pull away, though–

When I put my eye to the rent, the tiniest thread of light seemed to hang in the darkness beyond the plasterboard. Quick calculation told me there must be a small hole in the sidewall, which could only be the wall to my bathroom. When I hastily got up and went to the bathroom I saw that I'd inadvertently left the light on earlier.

A hole, came the plodding thought. *In the wall . . .*

A *peep*hole?

The notion seemed absurd but I could not forget my earlier impression: when I'd been bathing, I not only could've sworn I heard a human gust of breath *from behind the wall,* but I'd also been filled with the suspicion that I was being spied on . . .

No true logic could explain my next endeavor. Careful as ever–while back in the closet–I pulled chunks of the plasterboard away. The damage was already done, so damaging the wall further mattered little; I'd be paying for it regardless of the size of the hole. I suppose my motives at this earlier point were subconscious, but after I pulled away several more pieces of the wall, and shined into the hole the beam of my pocket-flashlight, I detected an area of space beyond that could easily be taken for a narrow walkway. Of course, it must be only a service passage, for access to pipes, electrical wires, and what not. Still . . .

I pulled away some more pieces until the hole was sizable enough to admit me, and then I crawled in.

Back on my feet, inside now, I approached the threadlike beam. Instinct, of course, put my eye to it posthaste.

I was looking directly into my bathroom.

It IS a peephole, came my first thought but then, *No, that's ridiculous!* The Hilman was obviously a respectable lodging-house. The hole could be explained by a number of circumstances: a simple construction flaw, or a nail-hole where a picture had been hung.

Deeper in the murk, though, I noticed *another* thread of light.

Taking every precaution not to misstep, I proceeded to this next light-beam and found, to my dismay, another hole, which looked directly into the bedroom of the suite next to mine.

I was at a loss for what to think just yet. A modest clatter came to my ears and, with my eye pressed to the hole, I noticed movement.

It was the maid I'd just spoken too, who'd only just this morning been pregnant. Solemn faced and dull-eyed she lethargically went about the task of making the bed and picking up. On a chair by the door, however, I noticed a small valise, which sat opened and showed that it was full of clothes. And on the dresser?

There sat a neat, beige Koko-Kooler hat, identical to that which William Garret had been wearing just this morn when I met him. Near the door, too, sat a briefcase that appeared all-too-similar to his.

But Garrett and his friend already checked out, I remembered.

Once the housekeeper had finished with the bed, she jammed the hat into the suitcase, close dit, then took it and the briefcase out of the room . . .

Only the baldest, most objective pondering occupied my mind now. I believed there were two more rooms on this side of the floor, and when I peered down–sure enough–I spotted two more of the tiny beams of light, signaling the existence of two more peepholes. Then, in the opposite direction of this hidden walkway, several more such beams could be discerned . . .

I kept my pocket-flash aimed down, on the floor. If this walkway did indeed exist for some ill intent–either for perversity, or remotely gaining knowledge of a lodger's potential valuables--there must be some mode of unobservable access. At the very end of the passage, on the floor, lay what could only be a trapdoor.

I opened it, spotted a rail-ladder, and without much conscious volition, found myself next taking the ladder down to the hotel's third floor . . .

Black as hackneyed pitch, this climbing-way was; I thought of the esophagus of some Mesozoic creature into whose belly I was venturing. A doorless aperture signaled the hidden passage paralleling the third floor, and it was through that I stepped to face a similarly dark hidden passage. A thread of light marked each of the floor's rooms but when I quickly looked into them, I noted only untenanted hotel rooms.

So–to the next floor I descended upon the ladder. The *second* floor. At the aperture I stepped into another hallway clogged with darkness made incomplete only by more intermittent threads of light. Here, though, I vaguely detected voices.

I let my shoes take me as slowly–and quietly–as possible to the first of the peeping-holes.

My vantage point only allowed me to view a wedge of the bland, clean room within, where I saw shelves of canned goods, sponges, buckets, towels, and other such items. The voices were distinctly female and seemed nonchalant. Several young women sat in the room, while I could only see slices of them; they appeared to be sitting on several couches. All were in some stage of pregnancy.

"–from Providence, I think, and he's quite handsome," one said.

"Oh, I know the one–he's kind of shy," observed another.

"And kind of rich! That's what I heard. That's why they won't take him."

My mind stalled as my eye remained to the hole. Could they . . . be talking about *me?*

A third, barely visible, contributed, "Oh, I know who you mean." A giggle. "I was upstairs looking in the peep-holes and saw him–you know–playing with himself!"

"No!"

"He pulled himself right off! In the bathtub–"

The other cackled while I, as might be expected, felt my spirit wilt. It could *only* be me they were talking about . . .

"–and you're right, he's quite a handsome one, but I liked the two others much better."

"The Boston men?"

"Yeah. I wouldn't have minded being made in the way from one of them."

"But, Lisa! Neither of them are very handsome now!" and then more giggling broke out.

I could only stare, more at my own bewildered thoughts than the scene within. This was outrageous, women who were more than likely maids spying on hotel customers. It was certainly actionable and I most certainly had a solicitor who'd be more than happy to sue, but . . .

What's the reason for all this? I had to wonder through my embarrassment and shock. Women weren't known to be peeping toms; that was an aberrancy reserved for men alone. And the reference to two *Boston* men could only mean Mr. Garret and Mr. Poynter. *Neither of them are very handsome now?*

"God, it's just so depressing having to do it when they're like that," came another observation. "I'm happy to be pregnant."

"Yeah. And they're not going to keep the Providence man."

"Why?"

"I told you, he's rich. The others are always fly-by-nights–no one knows they're here--but the Providence man–"

"He's no fly-by-night if he's rich. Someone would come looking . . ."

Even to contort my imagination to its maximum could not account for the words I was hearing, nor the outrageous evidence my curiosity had led me to uncover.

I moved to the next hole . . .

God in Heaven . . .

. . . and found myself looking at the most macabre scene I'd ever witnessed in my thirty-three years of existence . . .

Several bed mattresses lay on the floor, and in the corners were a few metal pans. "God, I hate this," snapped a woman's complaint. It was yet one more pregnant woman, this one rather dowdy and older. She'd perched herself on her knees, to tend to a man who lay on one of the mattresses.

Or, I should hasten to correct: the *remnant* of a man . . .

He lay dismembered, naked, scars at the bald nubs where his arms had been removed at the elbows and his legs at the knees. He was lean, pallid-skinned, and bearded, and what the pregnant woman was doing was crudely washing his groinal area with a sopping sponge. Her expression of distaste could not have been more vivid. "They just stink so! And, oh, the lice! I just hate this *so much!*"

"*You* hate it!" complained a second woman. "You don't have to *do* it!"

This objection had come from the forward-most mattress, on which lay a man in an identical state as the first, only he was clean shaven and blond-headed. I saw stitches showing at the nubs of his injuries. But the woman was not washing this one–she was engaged in an act of overt sexual congress, a look of loath on her face . . .

But this was a face I recognized:

Monica, I realized, *from the pier.* I'd just seen her a short time ago, in the stairwell and entering the perpetually locked door to the second floor.

Now I knew why that door was always locked.

What form of madness could explain what I was viewing? These unfortunate men had clearly been *made* into invalids. For them to have suffered *identical accidents?* Impossible. And their symptoms of amputation mirrored exactly those of Mary's brother, Paul. What foul auspication urged me to believe that these men had been *purposely* and *premeditatedly* invalidized for this obscene purpose?

The farthest edge of my vantage point showed me a third mattressed victim, and perched vigorously on his groin was another thin, young woman with her skirt hoisted to make her privates accessible. "Hurry, you stinking bastard," she muttered.

"This one shits himself, too," added the pregnant woman in her disdain. "He does it on *purpose.*"

"I do not!" blabbered the victim she was bathing. He seemed stricken with a vocal impediment. "I can't help it–"

"You know where the pans are!" the woman shrieked. "Maybe we'll stop feeding you for a while! See how you like that!"

"Leave him alone, Joanie," suggested the young woman with the hoisted skirt. "I have to do him next, and if he's upset he won't be able to. He'll wind up like Paul."

Like Paul, my mind droned.

I watched in the utter horror of it all, surely a scene from the Abyss. When this Joanie had finished with her congress, she grunted and rose, glaring down at her crippled purveyor. This poor man, after a minute or so, grotesquely rolled off the stained mattress, belly to floor, then hopped up onto the savaged ends of his limbs, after which he awkwardly ambled–doglike, on all fours–to one of the metal trays, to urinate. Meanwhile, the blond man began to gasp in something akin to tortured bliss while his unwilling partner, Monica, looked at him in a meld of bitter hatred and nausea. Indeed, it seemed some carnal warren in Hell that my eye had happened upon. *Incalculable,* I thought in the deepest despair. *Monstrous . . . ,* for the intent, macabre as it seemed, shone all too clearly.

It must have been some imp of the perverse which forestalled my immediate desire to extricate myself from this evil chasm–and from the very building itself–and just simply flee, when, next, I found myself looking instead into more of the appalling peeping-holes. Similar scenes of incomprehensible obscenity were my reward for this effort: men reduced to naked torsos, either lying inert on sullied mattresses or traversing the room on their butchered limb-ends. One lapped water from a bowl, again, like a dog. Room after room glared with these unfathomable scenes of grotesquerie. But in the next peeping-hole . . .

God, deliver me, I prayed.

This was no chamber of forced-conception. Instead, I spied

a room clinically adorned: medical supplies, IV bottles on stands, several elevated beds. Unconscious men with bandaged limbs occupied two such beds: one jibbered, drooling, in the clutches of nightmare, the other lay open-mouthed and utterly still. The man appeared youthful, yet I could clearly discern he had no teeth.

But the forward bed concerned me most.

On it lay Mr. William Garret, limb-ends similarly bandaged from his recent amputations. A tray of bloody surgical instruments, including a bone-saw, occupied a nearby tray, plus bottles clearly labeled CHLOROFORM. *This is a surgery suite,* I knew now, *hidden in the hotel on this floor which is always locked.* Cotton clogged Garret's mouth, and when suddenly he began to blink and shudder on the bed, a pregnant attendant came to his side, to comfortingly pat his shoulder. "There, there, you'll be all right," she calmly regarded him. "It's all for a reason that's more important than any of us." She tried to sound chipper. "And just think of all the pretty girls you'll be enjoying!"

Garret mewled beneath the cotton in his mouth. The cotton had tinged scarlet, and it was then I noticed a smaller stainless steel tray full of recently extracted teeth.

"He's coming to, doctor," claimed the pregnant nurse. "He'll need more pain antidote soon."

"Prepare the injection, please, Lucy."

The voice had arrived out of view, but next, I was not surprised to see a lab-coated Dr. Anstruther step up to the surgery bed. "It's best not to struggle, Mr. Garret, and far better to accept your new fate. Discard any yearnings of your former life. You'll get by much better, I assure you." He took a hypodermic from the nurse and eventually emptied it into an isolated vein. "The morphine sulphate is quite effective, and it will be administered regularly until no longer necessary—only a matter of days, really." With forceps, then, he removed the cotton from Garret's mouth. "And, as you've already deduced, I've extracted all of your teeth."

Garret's wasted expression turned to the doctor. "Whuh-whuh . . . why?"

"In time, you'll come to understand. Oh, and I'm happy to relate that I've examined your semen under the microscope and found an impressively high sperm-count and excellent motility. You're a preeminent candidate for sirehood."

Garret just stared, as if into an unreckonable cosmic gulf.

Anstruther turned to the nurse while jotting something on a board. "Lucy, the gentleman in Bed Number Two has unfortunately expired. He'll need to be disposed of, along with Mr. Garret's limbs."

"Yes, doctor."

"In a few days you'll be feeling much better," the doctor re-addressed Garret. "And like Lucy has already said, for some time to come, you'll be enjoying the company of many, many woman, most of whom are possessed of some considerable desirability. Such is the lot of a Sire, Mr. Garret. Do yourself a service and maintain the proper mental perspective. For so long as you remain virile you will remain alive, and in your quiet times, I'd advise you to solicit whatever god you may believe in."

The surgery-shocked and now toothless William Garret blabbered, "Look what you've done to me! Yuh-yuh-you're a *monster!*"

Anstruther smiled sedately. "No, Mr. Garret. You're fortunate in that you will never have to see the *real* monsters . . ."

When I forced my eye away from that Tartarean hole in the wall, I felt like a 100-year-old man. I staggered wide-eyed back the way I came, to the climb-way, where I had every intention of ascending back up to my room, securing my personal effects, and leaving this God-forsaken place posthaste. But when I got to the aperture which housed the ladder–

My heart slammed in my chest.

I heard footsteps. Climbing up.

Trying to cut the intruder off and make it up to my room

undetected possessed no probability at all. A subconscious directive, instead, took me back across the near lightless channel, to its opposite end, where I guessed–or prayed–that there might be an identical climb-way. *Please, Lord,* I beseeched in a mental groan.

Either my prayer had been answered or simple luck was with me, for, yes, there was another climb-way. I stepped in, grabbed the rungs, but before I could proceed upward–

"You, there," a voice called from the other end.

I didn't turn to look but instead tried to hide within the climbing-way's murk.

"Who is that? Nowry? Peters?"

I did not waste mental time considering why the male voice might be calling the name of a dead man, but it would be easy to suppose Nowry had other clan in town. Instead, I made my move. I did not climb up, I climbed down, for to return upstairs might sever any chance of escape. A similar hidden passage paralleled the first floor; I knew I needn't bother examining any of the peeping-holes here. *But there must be a way out, and I've got to find it!*

No door, though, or any other passage, became visible in the light of my pocket-flash . . .

Then I heard the footsteps coming down the ladder I'd just quitted.

To the passageway's opposite end I hastened, for where else could I go? I reasoned there had to exist some exterior access to these hidden crannies. For instance, how had my current pursuer gained the climbing-ways?

A door! I prayed. *There must be a door!*

But when I'd made this opposite end, I found no door; meanwhile, the footsteps echoed more loudly.

It was the sole of my shoe that found it: not a standing door, nor access panel, but a hinged plate-metal hatch. I opened it in relief but then gasped as my flash-lamp revealed details of the ungainly egression–a climb-way of ancient brick, fitted with a slime-coated iron ladder, leading straight down. It was with the staunchest resolve that I lowered myself down into its methanous depths, closed the hatch above me, and descended. My position forced a procession in total darkness; I half-expected at any moment to be lowering myself into an open sewer and the stercoraceous smells and matter that companioned them, but when my feet settled on solidity, I relighted my flash-lamp to find myself in still another passageway. My panic had skewed my bearings but an instinct told me the brick lined access proceeded north and south. For a reason unbeknownst to me, I took the southward way.

Flash in the lead, I walked for at least one hundred yards in the ill-smelling murk. I knew now, however, that this passage was not an out-of-service sewer line; no signs were extant of the expected residuum. *It's a tunnel,* I knew then, and as surely as if the words had been spoken aloud, *Zalen's* words seemed to echo in my head: *And my grandfather wasn't lying when he told Lovecraft about the network of tunnels under the old waterfront . . .*

I needn't define the extent of the chill that moved caterpillar-like up my spine. And of the hellish scene I'd witnessed back at the hotel, I could only assume that virile men with suitably favorable looks were being forced to inseminate local women, whose newborns were then sold to some illicit adoptive initiative. Why, though, was I more perturbed by what Zalen had told me, especially his cryptic final monologue: *In the story, what happened to outsiders who did too much nosing around?*

Now, it seemed, the most dreadful of circumstances had transposed my very self into Lovecraft's fictitious Robert Olmstead, the out-of-towner hellbent to escape the horrors of Innsmouth.

I could go to Zalen now, tonight, it came to me, *if I could only find the exit to this blasted catacomb . . .*

Minutes later, fate or God handed me said exit as a gift.

The tunnel emptied me near a rock jetty along the harbor's edge. A spectacular, frost-white moon hung behind intermittent clouds;

the water in the harbor sat still as glass. Gazing out over the twilit port, beneath the violet night, proved a supernal sight, but all else I'd witnessed was anything *but* supernal. More *phantasmal* than anything else, or more *iniquitous.* The very-normal appearing harbor, after closer scrutiny, was flecked by arcane maws. Mouths of rock-hidden grottos, and tunnel-exits exuding strange smells. No human instinct could prevent me from entering of such a maw . . .

More lichen and niter-crusted catacombs awaited me, several branching off from the main. I had to harness my sharpest sense of awareness, lest I easily be lost here. The leftmost tine in the fork was the one I chose. I kept my footing sure, only turning on the flash in brief increments in order to conserve its batteries. I didn't have to proceed far before the most hideous death-stench assailed me; a handkerchief to my face barely stifled its sickening noxiousness. Eventually, the tunnel emptied into vast cavern, the first glimpse of which nearly caused me to shriek and flee.

But how could I? I had to find out what *this* was . . .

A charnel house, I thought. *A makeshift sepulcher* . . .

It was mostly skeletons that heaped the obscene, dripping cavern, piles of them, some still dressed in scraps that had surpassed the effects of human decomposition. The bone-piles at the farthest end seemed the oldest, while those making their way–I believe–northwest, had been more recently deposited. Mid-heap, I found fewer skeletons and more bodies mummified. This was a *hillock* of human corpses that providence had seen fit to show me; hundreds, easily, had been left in here rather than in proper burying-grounds. *Why?* I choked on the question. Who could be responsible for this? The time-emptied eyes of skulls seemed to hollowly watch as I moved along the wretched boundaries of the mound, and when eventually I'd staggered to its end, I could've collapsed amid the stench and the unholy insinuation.

These–dozens of them–were obviously the sepulcher's most recently contributed corpses, and while most of the previous had been more or less "whole," the state of the constituents of the rotting, gas-bloated pile needed little conjecture as to their origins.

What primarily composed the ghastly heap of rot-covered bones, flesh-peeling skulls, and worm-rilled half-flesh were the evidence of *dismembered* human beings, each missing arms from the elbows and legs from the knees. Scraps of clothing lay among the human stacks like haphazardly tossed flags. I glimpsed too many suitcases and valises. A smaller pestiferous aggregation of severed arms and legs lay in vicinity.

An undercroft of corpses, a murder repository, I realized. And how long it had been here, I couldn't guess . . . and would never *want* to guess.

The sound of distant scuffling locked open my eyes and snapped off my flash. I back-stepped, praying I didn't fall, for the unmistakable sound of footsteps–and a more arcane unbroken grinding sound– seemed to be making its way toward the sepulcher. *But from where!* my thoughts demanded. My own path of entry lay behind me, while this sound came to my front. I ducked down behind a bunker of half-mummified cadavers just as a bobbing light could be seen.

Another entrance, I realized, from yet another of the stygian tunnels. I hid myself as still as the dead bodies about me, when eventually the light from an oil lantern bloomed, and the interloper appeared from an egress unseen till now. The figure pushed a wooden wheelbarrow whose contents was to be expected: the nude, stump-bandaged torso of the unfortunate post-surgery victim who'd expired in Dr. Anstruther's suite of horrors. Its half-limbs jiggled as the barrow made its way, and stacked upon its dead belly were several sets of other severed limbs, plus several suitcases. Then the barrow stopped and the lantern was set on the ground. The suitcases, first, were flung onto the pile, then the limbs, and then, with a flat grunt, the torso. Of the interloper himself I could only discern the frame of a man, and I could see he held no handkerchief over his mouth and nose. How he tolerated the charnel stench I couldn't imagine . . . until he raised the lantern once more, and the sizzling light revealed his face.

It was Mr. Nowry, whom just hours ago I'd glimpsed dead in an ambulance.

What ruse might explain this I didn't care to ponder, but when I first saw his pallid face in the light, I did, however minutely, gasp.

The figure froze, then turned. I froze as well, praying, and preparing to reach for my pistol . . .

The lantern swept this way and that, and by the grace of God its rays did not reveal my crouch. Eventually, Nowry returned to his wheelbarrow and exited the way he came.

I waited a full five minutes before even budging, then I rose and turned, snapped on my flash, and briskly marched for my own exit, but as I did so, I couldn't help but notice another oblong maw along the rockface. Yes, another tunnel.

Under no circumstance will I allow myself allow enter, I made the self-command but even before I was consciously aware, my feet were deputing me into this next rock-hewn entry. In spite of the grievousness of all I'd thus far seen, I had to wonder if Lovecraft himself had ventured into any of these tunnels, and then realized that he must have, for from where else could he have derived similar subterrene networks in masterpieces such as not only *Innsmouth* but "The Festival," "The Outsider," "The Rats in the Walls," and so on. I was now walking in the midst of a Lovecraft story, but knew that the obscene butchery taking place at the Hilman, and the cavern of horrors I'd just exited was no "story." Nevertheless, the indulgence of my curiosity outranked my capacity for reason.

I had to see what was at the end of *this* tunnel . . .

As my intermittent flash led me on, another odor assailed me but, thankfully, it was not one of death nor noxiousness. It was a strong odor with a distinct heft. The more deeply I traversed the tunnel, the more familiar the odor became:

The unquestionable odor of *fish.*

I lost my breath when the tunnel opened into a subterrestrial chamber many times the length and depth of the previous, and herein were many times the number of corpses.

These, though, were different . . .

Why no stench of rot and natural corruption? I pondered. *Why only the smell of fresh fish?* But when my eyes registered the *details* of what my retinas were registering, I felt sicker here than in the previous sepulcher.

The body mound stood *huge*–fifteen, twenty feet high and a hundred long. My sense of perception began to bend, though, as I squinted at the morass of bodies. *They-they . . . they're not altogether human,* I realized. *Some more, some less . . .* Almost all had been stripped of clothing, and their dead, nude skin seemed wax-white with tinges of an unwholesome green veined beneath the pallored translucence. Grievous physical deformities had twisted the lion's share of the corpses into outrageous misshapes; most were balding but all were possessed of wide-open and mostly blue-irised over-protuberant eyes. Closer inspection, then, showed me hands and feet in various states of elongation, while fingers and toes were clearly–

My God . . .

–webbed.

To the touch–and what compelled me to *touch* one of the things I can't imagine–the skin felt strangely moist, enslimed, and rubbery, semblant to the tactility of frog-skin. But the most chilling verification came next: at least half of these transfigured decedents had rows of slits along their throats. Like gills.

Just like the story, my thoughts grated. Could this possibly be true? *Madness,* I thought instead. Surely subterranean gasses known to accumulate in caverns and tunnelworks such as these could germinate hallucinations. It was my subconscious brain, tainted now by such leakages, that had me believing Lovecraft's greatest work was based on some fashion of biological fact. I stepped back from the gruesome heap of agape mouths; unblinking glassy orbicular eyes; pale, bone-bowed limbs; and ears that seemed to have partially or fully shrunk on hairless, semi-human skulls. Injuries, clearly, had been the cause of death for these malformed victims: wounds almost exclusively to the head and chest, and there was suggestion that a predominance of the wounds had been inflicted via gouges and punctures via talons and teeth.

I was too waylaid by this most monstrous and unbelievable sight to ponder any further. I had no choice but to hold my sanity in grave doubt but, next, just as in the first chamber of death, I heard the sounds of someone encroaching . . .

Again I doused my light and ducked behind a flank of piled half-human corpses when a light–no, several–were discernible. But voices as well, this time, two at least; and from the chamber's farthest cranny, the coming light enabled me to detect another rearward egress. By now I had to reason that the tunnelworks were extensive indeed. Two figures, then, one short, one taller, emerged, each bearing a candlefish torch. The sputtering, smoky flames threw cragged shadows everywhere, like a grim, kaleidoscopic nightmare.

"Gotta make it quick, son, like we'se always do," came a roughened, accent-tinted adult voice. "Ya never know when one'a their sentinels is liable to be snoopin' around."

"I know, dad," replied the obvious voice of a young boy.

"You cut out the biceps'n calves, like I taught ya, and I'll hack out the ribs'n bellies. Let's try'n get a whole lot in a little time, heh, son?"

"Sure, dad."

The smoky light easily revealed these new interlopers: Onderdonk and his young son. They must have discovered a tunnel of their own that gained them access without being visible to the town proper, where they clearly were not welcome. With a considerable skill, the boy flopped several corpses off the pile and within seconds was deftly butchering the meat off their arms and legs. Meanwhile, the father, with cleavers in each hand, systematically hacked lengths of ribs off more corpses and neatly cleaved out the abdominal walls. After they'd each administered to half a dozen or so of the dead half-human, half-batrachian monstrosities, they switched. Minutes later, they'd loaded the butchered wares into burlaps sacks.

"Good job, son," Onderdonk praised the lad. "Bet we got here more'n a week's worth'a meat for the smoker."

"I hope we make a lot of money, dad."

"That's my boy," the adult proudly smiled and patted his son's head. "It's God's way'a lookin' after God-fearin' folk like us, seein' to it that these half-blooders got the taste of fish'n good pork together. What choice we got seein' how them devil-lovin' Olmsteaders won't let us fish proper in their waters?"

"Yeah, dad. I'm glad God looks after us like this."

"We'se quite fortunate, son, and can't never forget it. Times're tougher for so many."

"But, dad?" The boy looked quizzical through a pause. "How come they don't rot and get to stinkin', you know, like in that other place?"

"It's 'cos them bodies in that other place is all pure-blood humans like us, but these here?" Onderdonk patted the slick greenish belly of a dead female whose face and bosom looked more toadlike, complete with warts. "All'a these here are 'least half-full'a the fish blood, like this splittail," and he callously cradled a wart-sheened breast. "This 'un here is likely fourth generation along with a whole lot of 'em–the one's ud already turned. But even first generation, boy, is enough to keep 'em from rotting proper, and bugs'n varmints don't go near 'em. It's their fish blood, see? That's what makes 'em never go to rot 'cos they cain't die, not unless they'se kilt deliberate or by accident."

"Oh," the boy replied. "That's kind'a . . . neat."

"Um-hmm. Now, help me fling these leavin's back."

With a drooping spirit, I watched from my discreted location as the pair heaved the butchered remnants up and over the mainstay of the piles, evidently to prevent any "sentinels" from ascertaining what had been done here.

"There," Onderdonk's whisper echoed. "Let's skedaddle . . ."

In the fluttering light, I watched them leave, sacks of pilfered meat flung over their shoulders.

But the sickness in my gut had long-since seized me: the stealings from this preternatural corpse-vault were clearly what Onderdonk passed off to unsuspecting customers as "fish-fed pork," a small portion of which now occupied my digestive tract. When safe to do so, I staggered away, all too aware that this was *not* the effect of hallucinotic gasses, and after retracing several yards back through the tunnel I'd entered in, I regurgitated the entire contents of my stomach.

Back on the rocky crags where the tunnel emptied, I fell to my knees in the relief of the fresh air and the simple sight of the normal world: the moonlight, the harbor, the boat docks and waterfront buildings. *The normal world, yes,* I thanked God, for I knew now how thin the veil was between that normality and utter, unnameable malignity. Who knew what other aberrant atrociousness the world hid just below its surface? I sat against the rock, listening to the water lapping against pier posts and shore–part of me quite paralyzed by my witness, not just *what* I'd seen but what it all *meant.*

I let the salt air flutter against my face and fill my lungs; I knew my body and my mind needed a few moments' rest before I could calculate the entails of my next move. I stared dumbly out into the pier-ringed inlet, watching silent boats rock gently in their slips, when my eyes found the barely noticeable rise of the sand bar . . .

Lovecraft's Devil's Reef, I mused. At least *that* had been pure invention. But who would believe the rest? And did *I* believe it?

At first I thought it must be a fleck of something in my eye but the more I stared the more convinced I became of something minuscule disturbing the late-night harbor's stillness.

A boat, I thought.

It was merely a small rowboat, and there appeared to be but one person aboard, oaring silently into the inlet. For several moments

I profaned beneath my breath when some clouds of deeper depths roved across the moon to darken the cryptic scene. It was likely only a crabber, or someone checking buoys, but I couldn't fight the temptation that it was more than that. When the clouds moved off, I saw that the meager skiff had been rowed deliberately aground on the longest finger of the sandbar, and its one-man crew had already debarked . . .

He's walking along the sandbar, I saw at once. *And . . . what's that he's carrying?*

Indeed, the distant figure was belabored by what seemed to be a sack that he was dragging along behind him. At that point, the veils of clouds moved fully away from the moon's radiant face, and suddenly the entirety of the harbor glowed in crisp, ghostly white light.

Even this far off, I could now see enough. The trudging figure wore what I was very sure had to be a long, greasy black raincoat and hood . . .

Zalen.

His progress halted when he came to the bar's point of greatest girth. Then he just stood there for many minutes, his head tilted down as if—

As if he's waiting for something, it morbidly occurred to me. *Waiting for something in the water . . .*

And then, from that same water, something did indeed emerge.

A figure, yes, but one unclothed and gleaming in a bump-ridden off-green hue. It stood lanky and lean, but long-limbed and with a head almost flattened and a face angled forward to a sharp point. Even from this distant vantage point I could fully detect the *hugeness* of its unblinking eyes; like crystalline globes, they were, aglitter from some stolid menace beneath. Eventually two more primeval faces rose slowly from the water, to reveal their full physiques to the moon, one decidedly female for it was well-breasted and much more widely hipped than the other two, whose maleness hung bumped and long at their groins. I was grateful that the distance did not afford me any further clarity of physical details.

The first one reached forward and took the proffered sack from Zalen . . .

I didn't need to be properly informed of the sack's contents for when the thing opened it up and looked in, the tiniest sounds eddied out, tiny, yes, but all-determinant.

The anguished wails of newborn babes.

More and more it was all coming true. How could I deny what my eyes were seeing? In all this ghastly insanity, what sane explanation could be winnowed out? On the sandbar the three monstrosities took their human booty and returned to the watery depths, while Zalen reboarded his small skiff and rowed away, and next–

thump!

I'm sure the sudden shock forced me to shout out. It was a spindly yet aggressive weight that landed on my person from above the outcropping where I sat: all blanched-white skin and a thin vicious face but strangely dead-eyed and veiled by an aura of long, dark, wispy hair. A thin hand snapped at once to my throat and began to squeeze with a strength greater than my own. It was the horror of the assault's suddenness in flux with my previous revelations that diced my thoughts. Instinct more than decisive mental computation triggered my own defensive maneuvers, feeble as they may have been. Only the merest sliver of volition registered, but I was able to discern that my banshee-like attacker was neither one of things I'd seen soliciting Zalen on the moonlit bar nor a living example of any of the part-human, part-monster hybrids I'd found in the earthworks. This instead was a hostile and purely human woman tearing at my throat with one hand and gouging at my eyes with the other. White teeth snapped open and closed an inch before my appalled face, but when I took closer note of *her* face, I screamed again, all that much more loudly. Surely the scream had been heard by anyone in proximity to the waterfront; it echoed cannon-like across the dark water.

The naked, feral thing clambering over me was Candace, the formerly pregnant prostitute who served as one of Zalen's obscene photo models. Divorced now of the bloated belly, her milk-swollen breasts looked too large for so thin a woman. Her post-childbirth death had darkened streaks under her eyes like tar-smears, and left her distended nipples the color of bruises.

"I saw you," I choked, "in the ambulance! You're dead!"

"Am I?" came a dry and strangely hacking reply. No gust of breath vented from her mouth when she'd said this, but worse was her facsimile of a laugh when she squeezed my throat even harder and reached back with her other hand to molest my groin.

"We-we could have a nice time together, sir . . ."

Of all the abominable things: she gently caressed my crotch with the gentleness of a lover, while the fingers of the other hand dug so deeply into my throat, I feared at any moment she'd be unseating my trachea and fully yanking it, adam's apple and all, out of my neck. It was obvious to me that death had enlisted her into the role of the aforementioned "sentinel."

If my screams had not alerted the whole of the waterfront's population, the ensuant pistol-shot most certainly did. This rejuvenated cadaver that had not too long ago been a wayward young woman named Candace was fully thrashed aside against the rocks. It had been a death-impulse that had unconsciously supervened my terror and slipped my hand into my pocket to withdraw the small Colt .32 repeater. The blind shot had struck at the vicinity of her left ear and took out a fair section of the right side of her cranial vault. I gasped in lungfuls of air as I watched the nude corpse impact the wall of rocks to our side. The report left me spattered with cool hanks of her convoluted gray matter bathed in ill-smelling blood which appeared blackish, not red, but traced faintly with threads of some alien constituent that glowed in the faintest pale green. In all, it smelled like heavy motor oil and fish.

The reckoning to make exit came immediately, for lights were snapping on along the waterfront edifices. Yet even having been divorced of a moderate portion of her brain, Candace falteringly rose and began to stumble after me but not before I'd gained enough ground to render her chase futile.

I hastened along the rock line, hoping for camouflage amongst dingy boulders and irregular light. Eventually I crossed the service road, slipped between a pair of drab-brick fish processors, and escaped that eldritch waterfront into the woods.

God, protect me, God, protect me, the vain prayer spun round my head. Only patches of moonlight managed to filter in to the fringe of woods; I daren't slip in too deeply lest I be blind–I didn't want to potentially reveal my position by having to rely on my flashlight, whose batteries were already growing dim. But as disoriented as my experiences had left me, I felt reasonably sure that my stilted progress was northerly–the direction necessary to lead me, first, to Mary's, and then, ultimately, out of town. I knew it would be miles of desperate walking to get to the next, safer, town. If only I could find a telegraph office–some were known to be operational twenty-four hours–or a rare telephone. But as I wended between stout trees, sometimes only inching along for lack of light, I knew there was a place I *must* go before any of that . . .

I should be getting close, it came to me after a half an hour's progress, and when I squinted between a pair of shabby buildings, I think I spotted to the cobbled lane before the fire station. *Yes!* There it was with its opened bay yet, oddly enough, not a soul could be seen in proximity. Just another twenty yards, then, and I knew I was collimating the unlighted rear wall of the building which housed Cyrus Zalen and his penurious neighbors. In fact, I could even smell the despair-compressed apartment row from the woods.

Dare I advance to the front door, or would it be better to tap on a rear window? Neither prospect enlightened me, but I knew that I *had* to confront this man. Zalen's apartment occupied the age-stained building's end; I crept ever-so-slowly around the side but then froze as if turned to a pillar of salt like Lot's wife Edith . . .

Behind several twisted, century-old trees out front, I could see the shadowed edges of *men.*

My heart could've burst when, from behind, a hand rough as sandpaper clamped over my mouth and I was yanked back into the woods as if jerked by a tether. One of their "sentinels," no doubt, had espied my encroachment. Smothering, I wrestled in vain against a wiry yet ferociously strong shadow. All my breath jettisoned from my chest when I was slammed to the ground.

"Don't make a sound, you fool!" shot a sharp, desperate whisper. I managed to extract my pistol, pointing it upward, but then the faceless shadow continued, "You pull that trigger, we're both dead."

I knew at once, from the voice, it was Zalen.

"Shhh!"

The shabbily-raincoated form didn't fear my weapon at all; instead, he left me where I lay, to peek stealthily past the tree we were both, in essence, hiding behind. When he returned, his whisper seemed calmed.

"You're lucky they didn't see you. Shit, we both are."

"What are you–"

Quiet anger. "They're staking out my room, man! They're waiting for me, and they're after you too, you idiot. You almost gave us away, and by now I probably don't have to tell you what they'd do to us. You wouldn't be hiding in the woods yourself if you didn't know."

The frantic slugging of my heart began to abate. "Sentinels. That's what Onderdonk called them."

"Anyone part of the town collective is in on it," Zalen whispered. "They serve *them.*"

"I saw you!" I whispered back as fiercely. "You're telling me that Lovecraft's story is all true! What's more–*now*–is I *believe* that!"

"How could you not?" Did the slinky figure chuckle? "You must be coming from the waterfront, where I *told you* not to go after dark.

Between your snooping around and my big mouth . . ."

"Now I know why so many women here are pregnant--I saw what they're doing on the second floor of the Hilman!" I grated. "They're crippling men and using them to–"

"Sure, think about it. Anstruther's one of the bigwheels. He cuts off their legs so they can't run away, cuts off their arms so they can't fight, and pulls their teeth so they can't bite the girls. The initiative is to keep every woman in the collective perpetually pregnant. Whenever some guy's passing through, if he's young, from a good bloodline, yeah. That's what they use 'em for. That's what the things want–newborn babies . . ."

"For sacrifice! It's abominable!"

Zalen rolled his eyes in the moonlight. "Oh, man, you're really dense. This isn't some occult witchcraft thing. It's *science.* That's all Lovecraft wrote about when you read between the lines. The more newborns the town can give them, the happier they are. So they reward the collective."

"*Reward?*"

"This is a *fishing* town, Morley. They reward us with an abundance of fish. Before the New Way, back in the old days, they'd also give us gold."

I stared. "Just like in the story."

"Just like the story, man, yeah. They don't do the gold anymore because it got too conspicuous. The town doesn't need it. All the gold did was make people lazy. Now it's all the resource, *fish.* For the last ten years this little piss-ant fishing village has become the most profitable seafood port in the country. We give them what they want, they give us what we want: prosperity. And anytime out-of-town boats try to sneak in and throw nets or drop lines–" Zalen chuckled again. "The boats sink and the people on 'em are never seen again. Hate to think what they do to the poor bastards . . ."

The ramifications now were sinking into the very meat of my soul. "They," I sputtered in disgust. "Lovecraft's Deep Ones, the

Dagonites."

"Naw, that's just a bunch of names he made up, Morley. We don't know *what* they're called"–he shrugged–"so we just call them fullbloods, or the *things*. Lovecraft learned enough, though. He was first here in '21 but he didn't find out anything, but in '27?" Zalen's vagabond grin beamed in the dark. "You're kind of like him, you know? He came here 'cos he liked the sights, but then he started snooping. They let him leave because they didn't really know who he was. But that goddamn *story*." He sighed futilely. "They've been here ever since Obed Larsh brought some of the crossbreeds from the East Indies. And he summoned the fullbloods with some kind of beacon the islanders gave him before they all got wiped out."

Beads of cold sweat trickled down my face, like bugs crawling. I could only stare at the horrendous gravity of what he was saying, and what I had no choice but to *believe*. "In the story federal agents and naval vessels destroyed them, so why–"

He cut me off with an offended smirk. "That's about the only part he made up–drama, man. Yeah, I know, they torpedoed the reef but you already know there never *was* a reef. What Lovecraft got right– *too* right–was the history. It was a true-life tale of social decadence and moral collapse. They have their own power hierarchies just like us; our leaders change and so do theirs. For the longest time they encouraged crossbreeding between their species and humans, but it was all just for the sake of lust. A human with mixed blood would change over time–things in every cell in their bodies–and eventually they'd become so similar to the things that they wouldn't die. They had all the poor saps in town believing that after they'd changed over completely, they'd go to the water and live in harmony with them forever, but all the things really did was use the crossbreeds for slavery. But even after they'd changed, they were still part human, and they'd bring their human flaws with them. Addiction, dishonesty, treachery. It got to the point where the part-human crossbreeds began to taint *their* society. So what did they do? Same thing we did after

Herbert Hoover, same thing Russia did after the corrupt Czars. They changed their power hierarchy; they cleaned their own society up by getting rid of the corruptive element–human blood. There were no *federal* troops that ever came here to wipe out all the crossbreeds. The things did that themselves–it was a wholesale slaughter, about 1930, I guess. They came up out of the water one night and murdered every single person in town who had any of their blood in them." Zalen paused on a reflection. "Lovecraft would've loved it. They were *doing* what he believed: wiping out the living products of sex between races–or in this case–between *species.*"

As I put my frantic thoughts to words, they seemed to grind out of my throat. "The first cavern I found via the tunnelworks you told me of, it was full of rotting, dismembered corpses. *Rotting,* I tell you; it was *pestiferous.* The air was nearly *toxic.*"

"That cavern is for the Sires that die."

"*Sires?*"

"The guys they dismember and hole up on the second floor. Every woman in the collective comes in there every night until they're pregnant, but you've already figured that out. Well, they don't live forever, you know, or sometimes a Sire becomes impotent. There's no use for them so the town elders kill them and let their bodies rot with all the others."

More and more things were making a revolting sense. "And the largest of the grottoes, full of so many more bodies, are the crossbred victims of the genocide in 1930?"

"That's right. They don't rot because their flesh is pretty much immortal. Even if you kill them by violence, they never decompose. Where do you think that weirdo Onderdonk and his kid get all that fresh meat?" and then he, ever-so-faintly, laughed. "Come on," he whispered next. "Let's get out of here."

Why I suddenly felt allied to this man–this baby-killer–I had no clue. It was all circumstantial, I suppose. Through dapples of moonlight, I followed him well away from the back of the apartment row, until he came to a barely perceivable trail. I had no choice but to follow. It occurred to me that Zalen's primitive interpretations reflected some of the most recent scientific breakthroughs all too chillingly. Certainly the last decade had trumpeted the works of the Darwinist Englander William Bateson, who'd founded and named this remarkable new science called genetics: the idea that microscopic cellular constituents pass on *hereditary* traits within a species, and other constituents known as *mutagens*, be they accidental or deliberate, can alter said traits. In addition, famed laureate microbiologist Hattie Alexander had just this month proven the viability of a miraculous anti-pneumonia serum through the manipulation of what she calls a *genetic-code* found within the viral cells themselves. If the fund of human knowledge was only now making such discoveries, how much superior might Zelan's *things* be with regard to similar sciences?

I was too afraid to contemplate the notion further.

We appeared to be veering northwest now, and for the first time, the woods felt safe. But in Lovecraft's story, there *was* no safe, and his own version of Sentinels could be hiding anywhere, ready to overhear forbidden talk—

And ready to report back . . .

"How many were killed all told?" morbidity forced me to ask.

"The crossbreeds? About a thousand, I think," Zalen said. "Lots of them were fourth and fifth generation. They were living in the ruins along Innswich Point–the old waterfront. When the government *did* come, the whole town was squeaky clean. No riff-raff, ya know? That's how we came to qualify for the federal rebuild."

Something even *more* morbid spidered along my awareness. "Where," I dared to ask, "are Mary's children? She told me she's had eight–and expectant of a ninth–but I only witnessed *one* child around her property."

Zalen huffed as he proceeded. "No women in the collective are allowed to keep *all* their children. They're only allowed to keep one–

their first."

"I already know what happens to the others," I all but choked. "But I need to know *specifically.*"

"Oh, do you, now?"

"You called me dense for assuming the newborns are sacrificed in an occult rite. If that's not the case then what exactly *are* these things doing with all those newborns?"

"How do I know, man?" he smirked back at me. "I'm not one of them, remember? I was never allowed into the town collective–I'm considered an outcast."

But not so much an outcast to be excluded from serving these things, I reasoned. I loathed this man–for what he was and what I'd seen him do–but I knew I mustn't rile him. His information was too valuable, and it may well serve to help assist my escape. An escape I was determined to make with Mary . . .

"The babies that don't come out right," he went on in grave monotone, "I guess they use for food. Candace's kid, for instance. She had it today, and it was all messed up from the horse she was shooting–I warned the bitch–but she lucked out in the end. She died while she was having it."

"Only in a manner of speaking," I begged to differ. "That *dead* girl almost killed me on the waterfront tonight."

"Oh, so that explains the shot I heard–"

"Indeed, it does. I killed her, but she was already dead. I also saw Mr. Nowry disposing of bodies in the first cavern. He was dead in the same ambulance with Candace only hours before."

Zalen shrugged. "They don't do it much, only when they need extra workers–"

"You're talking about raising the dead!" I exclaimed.

"Keep your voice down!" he sneered back at me. "And I'm talking about a lot more than that. You better pray you never have to see one of the fullbloods, but don't be fooled. They may *look* primitive but they're superior to humans in every way. And, yeah, they have some sort of reagent that can restore life to people who've died under certain circumstances. They've always had it. It's more of that cellular stuff . . ."

More genetic science, I realized but my thoughts kept deflecting. I simply couldn't get her off my mind. "How long . . . has Mary been part of this town collective?"

"Five years, maybe, six years. Who cares? And speaking of your precious Mary . . ." Zalen slowed amid the woods, and urged me westerly. Suddenly my eyes bloomed in frosty moonlight; I was looking at something I'd already seen . . .

Where the modest lake had earlier gleamed in sunlight, now it shimmered in the light of the moon. I glimpsed figures along the lake's shore.

Zalen held me back behind some trees before I had chance to blunder forth. "Not a sound," Zalen warned.

Verbosity couldn't have been further from my mind; instead, it was *witness.* Several dozen women stood in a semi-circle just at the water's edge, and I must say, this first glimpse of them made me think singularly of occultism. The late hour, the moonlight, and the location only exacerbated a namelessly sinister provocation in my mind . . .

The women wore primal robes whose color was indistinguishable in the intense moonlight, but what *could* be distinguished were fringed panels of fabric segmented by lighter-colored stitch-work. Within these segments more elaborate embroidery could be seen: symbols quite glyph-like and the oddest designations of geometry that, when looked upon to stridently, caused my head to ache. Were the angles of the horrific geometrics actually *moving?* Each woman, too, held a candle before her–a candle whose flame burned *green*–and I thought I could hear the faintest chimes, the notes of which instilled in me, to the core of my very guts, a feeling of uncontemplatable dread via the idea of utter *absence.* Absence of light, absence of benevolence, absence of morality, absence of all things *sane.* Even more softly than the sourceless chimes there came to my ears a vocal diaphony that made me want to fall to my knees and be sick: a discordant and cacodaemonically unstructured sequence of words which sounded like:

"Ei . . ."

"Cf'ayak vulgtuum . . ."

"Ei . . ."

"Vugtlagln, sjulnu . . ."

"Ei, ph'nglui, hkcthtul'ei . . ."

"Wgah'nagl fhtagen–ei . . ."

"Ei, ei, ei . . ."

The perverse chants seemed to grow lighter rather than louder, but for some reason the more difficult this evil song was to hear, the more impact it had on my mind, a veritable *pressure,* a *tactuality* against my face. Yet as sick as I felt, I felt something else concurrently: a most powerful carnal arousal.

"Keep back," Zalen whispered. He forced me to crouch lower. "This lake empties into the bay . . ."

The solemnity of that information didn't at first occur to me. My vision, instead, remained hijacked to these macabre, robed women. The chorus was chanted again when all the women at once dropped their robes and stood nude.

Nude, I had no choice but to observe, *and pregnant.*

All the while, the chant seemed to compress my brain within the confines of my skull. It was sordid and erotic, seeing this in such a manner that I could not look away–indeed, it was evil. Most of the women appeared in their twenties, but I did make out Mrs. Nowry and some others more middle-aged. All of them, then, one by one, tossed their queerly green candles into the water, and I could take an oath that as each stick of wax sunk beneath the surface, the green flame was not extinguished, and at the same time my eyes seemed to acclimate more intensely to this tinseled night: the moonlight grew sharper, brighter, and with this, my vision grew more acute. Even

from this considerable distance, I could make out refined details of
each gravid woman. I could see the pores on their white skin, the
minute line between each iris and the whites of their eyes, the papillae
of each and every nipple, and the fine traceries of venousity within
each milk-soused breast. Eventually all of them lowered to the muck
of the lake shore, and what took place then I'll only distinguish as an
obscene bacchanal of the flesh, a libertine debauch intent on mutual
satiation akin to the Isle of Lesbos. I shouldn't have to specify, either,
that one of these concupiscent attendants was Mary herself . . .

My eyes held rapt on the orgiastic scene, and for a time I thought
that even a gun to my head couldn't make me look away even in the
self-knowledge averting my eyes was the only Godly thing to do.
But it was Zalen, not God, who urged my surcease.

"It's coming out now—"

"It?" I questioned in the slightest whisper.

"We're not going to be here to see it. Believe me, Morley, you
don't want to see it . . ."

He hauled me back into the woods just at the same moment a
figure began to rise from the lake.

My head thankfully cleared with proximity. "What—what *was*
that, Zalen?"

"It was one of them—what did you think?" the long haired,
greasy-coated man chided.

One of them, I thought. *A fullblood . . .*

"One of the hierarchs, but there could be others about too."

I winced at the madness. "That was an occult rite we just
witnessed, Zalen. After all I've learned, and everything you told me
that happens to be true, there has to be more . . ."

"Of course there is," the spindly vagabond retorted. "But all that
shit out there by the lake?" He seemed amused. "It's just tradition,
Morley, it's just ritual; it means nothing. All it proves is how much
lower mankind's mentality is; the only way we could ever really
relate to the fullbloods—even back in Obed Larsh's time—is through

ignorant ritualism like this . . ."

"Just a veneer," I speculated, for so much occultism in the Master's work was just that. "Is that what you're saying?"

"You hit it right on the head. What looks like devil-worship and simple paganism is just the icing on a very different kind of cake."

The analogy, trite as it may have been, validated my assurances now. I followed Zalen unknowingly for a time, my mind too active with a plethora of conjectures. "But all societal systems ultimately have a defined purpose," I insisted. "If this occultism is veneer–or 'icing' used to cover something else up . . . what *is* the something else?"

"You ask too many questions. I warned you about that," he said. "We have to get out of here, that's all. You've got money and a gun, and I've got the way out. If we're lucky, we might make it."

"Don't tell me you've got a motor-car," I nearly exclaimed.

"Sure, I do–er, I should say, I know where we can get one," he supplemented with a chuckle. "The Onderdonks have a truck. That's where your gun comes in."

For whatever reason, this decidedly promising news did not reduce the regard of more of my questions. "You could've stolen their truck anytime in the past. Why is escape on your mind *now?*"

"I told you," he smirked back in spattered moonlight. "Because they're onto us now. Someone overheard me talking to you earlier–"

"So that's it, a breach of the secrecy everyone here must adhere to," I surmised. "More, more of the story."

"Because Lovecraft's story wasn't really a story. I told you that too. Most of it's true. And now we've got to live with it–or die."

I continued to follow his footsteps, still confounded and–why, I'm not sure–enraged more than terrified. The smell of slow-cooking meat waxed dominant; it sifted down the narrow trail to tell me that Onderdonk's property drew near. I was appalled to admit that the aroma–even in knowing as I did the origin of the meat–was delectable. It also appalled me that Zalen, an inveterate thief, criminal, and, worse, one who was a willing party to infanticide, represented my greatest chance of escaping with Mary.

"Mary," I said next. "She must go with us."

"You've got to be kidding me!" he snapped.

"I insist. I have a great deal of money, Zalen. It would behoove you to accommodate my indulgence. Mary, her son, her brother, and her stepfather will be joining our escape."

At this he actually laughed. "Her and the kid, maybe. But Paul's deadweight; he's a Sire who went impotent. Only reason he wasn't killed and taken to the tunnels is 'cos she begged the hierarch." His next chuckle could've passed for a death-rattle. "And the stepfather? Haven't you been listening?"

"I can't fathom you, Zalen. Mary's stepfather is aged and rife with infirmities. It would be un-Christian of us to abandoned the old man."

"The stepfather is a crossbreed!"

I gawped at words as though they were fragments of shrapnel. "But-but, I thought–"

"Crossbreeding between the two species was made illegal by the new hierarchs, so–"

"So all the existing crossbreeds were exterminated in the concerted genocide," I'd already gathered. "Which doesn't explain why Mary's stepfather is still alive."

Zalen stopped to face me, with that nihilistic grin I was now all-too-accustomed to. "You'll love this part, Morley . . . but are you sure you wanna hear it?"

"Don't toy with me, Zalen. Your psychological parlor tricks are quite juvenile if you'd like to know the truth. So kindly tell me that– the *truth*."

"We don't know exactly how their political system works but we think it's several of them in charge and there's one who's more powerful than the others."

"It's called an oligarchical monarchy, Zalen. The senior hierarch would suffice as the sovereign, akin to the Soviet Union of today, or this man in Germany, Hitler."

"Yeah. The sovereign. The sovereign's hot to trot for your wonderful little Mary. How do you like that? He's got kind of a *thing* for her. That was probably him back there at the lake. Don't worry, it won't fuck her–it's not allowed to . . . but it'll probably do everything else."

The information sickened me but also made me feel haunted. Thoughtlessly, I seized my handgun and turned to head back to the lake.

"You really are an idiot, Morley," I was told amid more laughter. He'd grabbed my arm and thrust me back. "Even if you did get a clear shot at it, there'd be a hundred more after you in two minutes. They'd *sniff* us out. We wouldn't stand a chance"

I leaned against a tree, gripped by a harrowing despair. "You're telling me that Mary's stepfather was spared from the genocide because–"

"–because Mary begged the hierarch not to kill him. She agreed to keep the old stick in hiding, at her house." Zalen nodded. "Hate to think what she had to do to get *that* favor."

I could've killed him on the spot for saying such a thing, but I knew there was truth behind it; desperation led to desperate acts. Instead, I collected my senses and continued to follow him. "What about those who aren't in Olmstead's town collective?"

"Rejects, like me, are left alone as long as we don't tell outsiders what's going on here, and as long as we don't leave."

"Those things can't possibly be everywhere," I declared. "With a modicum of forethought, I'd suspect that escape would be easily achievable."

"Sure, you'd *think* so," he counted, "but why do you think nobody does? Why do you think Mary's still here? It's not because she wants to be, I can tell you that. None of us do."

"Fear, then?"

"Uh-huh. In the past people–mostly women–have tried to escape. They just can't handle giving up their babies. But every single one has been brought back"–now Zalen's expression turned cold–"and made an example of. There are a whole lot more of those things than anyone can guess. If you leave, they'll track you down the way a bloodhound catches a scent, Morley. They travel along any existing waterway, and they're very fast."

I had no choice but to postulate, "So even if we do manage to get out of here, you don't deem our chances of success to be very high."

"No, but when they're on a rampage like they are now, if we *don't* try, we're dead by morning for sure."

Waterways, hunting a scent, I thought. If we made it back to Providence, I'd install Pinkerton's men round the clock. Either that or I'd relocate to a place so far removed from any waterways.

"There's the truck," Zalen whispered just as the trail had navigated us to an opening in the woods just behind Onderdonk's property. The aroma of slow-cooking meat hung dense. Several shacks sat teetering in shadows; betwixt two of them I spied a pickup truck that looked as dilapidated as everything else. The only sound that came to my ears was that of pigs chortling.

"Onderdonk's had those same pigs for years," came Zalen's next snide remark, "but they're just for show. I'll bet that hillbilly and his kid haven't really cooked pork for a decade."

"But where is he?" I queried. "The place looks abandoned."

"They probably went to bed after they put the meat in the smoker," he suspected, and pointed to the rows of propped-up metal barrels which sufficed for the cooking apparatus. "That's good for us ... but get your gun out just in case."

I obeyed the instruction and followed him into the overgrown perimeter. We ambled forth with great care, so not to snap a single twig. Moonlight and shadows diced the various shacks into wedges of light and dark; several sets of small eyes glittered at us when the pigs in the sty took note of us. An owl hooted, then went silent.

"That seems irregular," I commented of the burlap sacks near the smokers. "Those sacks appear to be full. I saw Onderdonk with my own eyes, carrying the sacks out of the cavern after he and his boy butchered a number of the crossbred corpses."

Zalen opened a sack; in it were hanks of freshly butchered meat. "Yeah, and if the meat's still in the bags, then what the hell is . . ."

The question didn't necessitate completion. I suppose, deep down, I already knew before we raised the lids of the smokers. I shined my flash inside, then we both recoiled.

Smoke billowed up from Onderdonk's pink-blistered face, while tendrils of it hung off the hair on his scalp. More smoke, as well, issued from the mouth agape in horrific death; the eyes had curdled cloudy white. A powerful, pork-like aroma spread a ground fog throughout hodgepodge of shacks. Another smoker sealed the fate of Onderdonk's boy–a pitiable sight, indeed. The lower body-weight, and the probability that the boy had been "cooking" longer than his father, was demonstrated by the fact his eyesockets were filled with bubbling humors. Steam from the poor lad's poached brain keened from his sinuses and ears.

"God save us," I croaked.

"The fullbloods got to them," came Zalen's hopeless appraisal, "which means they may still be here."

The prospect seized my heart like a vulturine claw and squeezed. We all but slithered in the direction of the motor, eyes never blinking. But, still, my questions remained in a maelstrom. "Previously, you told me that women made pregnant were allowed to keep their firstborn, but the others must be relinquished to the fullbloods."

"Yeah? So what?"

"But you also told me that you yourself fathered Mary's third or fourth child. What kind of a treacherous cretin could deliver *his own child* to those things in the water?"

"I didn't have anything to say about it, Morley. We don't have a *choice* here–don't you get that? If I'm 'treacherous,' then so is your beloved Mary."

I wouldn't hear of it. I *knew*, I knew to the marrow of my *soul*, that Mary's misgivings were levered upon her; if she did not comply, her son, brother, and stepfather would be made fodder for the fullbloods.

"And the kid we had was an accident," he went on. "I suppose back then I actually loved her–before she joined the collective."

I winced at the excuse. "Only the unGodliest of men could proclaim to *love* a woman he was prostituting out like a commodity."

"You don't know what you're talking about," and then came a snicker. "And I don't believe in God anyway."

"I should say that's obvious–"

"So if your God really exists, you're gonna have to do a lot of praying to get us out of this." We both arrived at the truck; in the back bed stood two cans of petrol. Ducking down, Zalen took one and carefully emptied it into the vehicle's fuel tank. "And," he went on, "you can *pray* that this hunk of junk starts..."

"One last question first," I importuned and gripped his shoulder. My curiosity burned like a brand-iron. "Answer what you refused to answer before."

"Come on, Morley, we have to–"

"I insist! You said that the ritualism is just veneer founded in ignorant traditions of old: occultism used as 'icing' to cover something else."

"Yes!"

"So what about the babies? What about the sacrifices? If the sacrifice of newborns isn't an *occult* oblation, then what else *can* it be?"

"It's not sacrifice, for God's sake. They want the newborns to study them–to study *us*. Their brains, their cells, their blood–everything, to see how they grow. Like what I said before–the microscopic things in every cell that make us what we are . . . *that's* what they study, *that's* what they experiment with."

"Their understanding of the genetic sciences must outweigh

129

ours a thousandfold," I said. "So that's it."

"Yeah. Sacrifices to the devil? Black magic? It's just a bunch of what my grandfather used to call codswallop. Ornamentation, Morley, to fool the ignorant masses: *us.*"

It was with little positivity that I contemplated the potential of his explanation. Based on the little I'd read I knew that, in theory, the study of human genes (particularly human genes still in developmental stages such as infancy) could not only enhance understanding of human life but could *alter* human life. I was forced, next, to ask, "What is the purpose of their studying us on a genetic level, Zalen?"

"That's the worst part," he said. "They hate us, Morley. They want to wipe us out, but not by brute force."

"With what, then?"

"With disease, deformity, sterility."

"Of course," I croaked, aware now of the ramifications. "Via research and experimentation on the newborns, the fullbloods could identify our biological vulnerabilities and produce viruses, malignancies, and contagious disease mechanisms that could lay waste to the human race from a multitude of angles."

"That's right. That's what they want to do eventually–"

"And you're helping them!" I snapped.

He frowned in the moonlight. "I thought I was helping *you.* I'm helping you and your precious Mary escape. Remember that." He turned then to the bedraggled vehicle. "Start praying, Morley. Pray to your God that this has a starter button instead of a keyed ignition . . ."

I actually did pray for that, but before the prayer was done, I'd leapt back, yelling in fright, for when Zalen opened the truck's dented and paint-faded door, he didn't *lean* in, he was *pulled* in–

–by a pair of long, thin, bizarrely jointed and musculatured arms with hands more resembling the forepaws of a frog, but with slick, webbed digits nearly a foot in length. I never saw its face, though I clearly understand what *it* was by the pungent smell which gusted from the truck when Zalen opened the rusted-patched door. It was the smell of a *fish*-pile tinged by the earthy stench of creek scum. Creek scum, too, was what the thing's skin looked like. It took moments in these wedges of shadow for me to compose reactive thought. I did seem to see its bump-pocked sickly green skin *shine* as if wet, and as the commotion ensued within the truck I also heard wet *sounds*, *slopping* sounds, and then sounds which were more refined and more ghastly.

Only the word *evil* could describe what I heard next, though to make direct simile I'd have to say it sounded like someone dislocating the joints of a raw chicken, only the "chicken," in this case, was Zalen. A heftier tearing sound followed, after which came a great, wet *splat* as all of the long-haired malcontent's internal organs were tossed out of the truck, and after that came the addict's destitution-worn black rain jacket.

Then came the arms, uprooted at the shoulder sockets.

Then the legs.

It's taking him apart, piece by piece, I realized.

And last came the torso, though Zalen's genitals appeared to be absent from the groin. I could only hope that the chewing sound I heard from the truck was my imagination.

I do not consider myself a coward, however, for not attempting to intercede with my pistol, for what you must understand is that the above dismantling of Cyrus Zalen expended only a matter of a few seconds. Instead, I rolled behind a rotted tree stump of considerable breadth. Reflex more than my conscious brain directed my positioning; I lay on my belly, both hands outstretched gripping my weapon, doing my best to establish a firing lane over the area I knew the creature must venture into if it were to pursue me. Shooting eye lined up over the weapon's small sights, I waited.

And waited.

Come out! I pleaded.

No significant movement could be detected within the truck, though I believe I noticed *minor* movement. A moment later–and

Edward Lee

for *only* a moment–the faintest greenish luminescence seemed to fluoresce within, and I could only judge that it was coming from the passenger side of the vehicle's interior. A second later, it was gone.

What guided me to re-examine Zalen's torso I can't imagine, but as I did so I made the sickening revelation that the cad's head was no longer in connection with his neck. Why had the batrachian monstrosity within ejected everything but the head?

Something arched in the darkness, thumped, then rolled to answer my question.

Zalen's head.

The head grinned in a manner that mirrored Zalen's snideness to perfection. The whites of its eyes, in a faintness that was less than minute, glowed with the same greenish ghost-light I'd noticed in the truck. "Think about what you're doing, Morley," came Zalen's corroded voice, yet a wet, slushy titter now companioned the words. "You don't have enough bullets to take them on, but you *do* have choices."

The dead words wracked me in a near-paralysis. Zalen's head chuckled when I shakingly aimed the gun at its brow. I noticed, too, that the torn and bloody stump of the neck glowed phosphorically with the thinnest tendrils of whatever netherworld-elixir had been administered into it–the reagent, I presumed, that had also reanimated Mr. Nowry, Candace, and Lord knew how many others.

"What . . . choices?" I finally managed.

"Join Olmstead's town collective–"

"Bombast," I said in spite of my revulsion and fear. "I will not be a party to infanticide, nor will I aid and abet the enemies of my race."

"Jesus, man. If you don't join them, you're dead. Oh, sure, you might take down a few of them with that peashooter of yours, but they'll get you eventually." The severed head winked. "And when they do, it won't be a pretty sight."

"I'd sooner shoot myself."

"Well, that's the only *other* choice you have. If you're not gonna

132

join them then you better do yourself a big favor and put that gun to your head right now and pull the trigger, Morley. That thing in the truck just pulled me apart in less time than it takes to bat an eye. You have any idea how much that *hurt?*" and then the dead mouth bayed wet, mushy laughter.

When I looked up, I spotted the silhouette of the thing standing just outside the truck now, staring at me in great attendance. The eyes which shined in the darkness were gold-irised and seemed the size of adult fists. Its evilly webbed hands hung down well below the joints that sufficed for its knees.

"Of course," the wretched head continued, "if you're gonna kill yourself, you'll need to kill Mary first–"

"Mary?" I exclaimed.

"If you don't join the collective, they'll do things to her that will make the Holy Inquisition look like a couple of kids playing in a sandbox. They'll torture the daylights out of her, Morley, with their chemicals and their tools, and then they'll kill her, and then? They'll bring her back just to do it all over again."

"Shut up!" I yelled and put the gun to the head's eye.

"But none of that'll happen if you join the collective. You'll have your Mary, happily ever after."

Tempting as they may have been, I knew that I could not fall prey to his promises. If I agreed, they would kill me just the same, for what I knew. I prevaricated, biding time–there was still the fullblood at the truck to deal with–"Let me think about this," I delayed–but then I looked back to the truck and saw that the heinous, scum-skinned creature was no longer there.

"Too late," Zalen intoned with a chuckle.

If was from behind that the slime-gloved hand came round and encompassed my entire face; I was hauled back, unable to breathe, and my pistol fell out of my hand. The foot-long fingers encased the full of my head, and thin as they may have been they exerted such force that I knew only seconds would be required before my skull burst like a pressured gourd. Zalen's execrable head continued to cackle as my struggles grew more enfeebled; worse, the aberration's other flagitious hand was slipping its way beneath my belt and into my trousers. What I suspected is had used Zalen's genitals for were about to be duplicated with my own.

"Looks like your God hit the road, Morley," hacked another splattering laugh of the evil head. "Can't say that I blame Him . . ."

It was almost merciful the way my consciousness dimmed just as the marauding hand clasped my genitals and began to twist. Would my skull erupt before I ultimately smothered? I felt the thin, boney fingers tightening, slickened by frog-slime. It seemed to temper itself then, as though it would uproot my privates and collapse my head simultaneously; but as I felt what I was certain were my last heartbeats, the abomination released me as if electrically shocked, leapt upright onto its hideous feet, and released a bellow so cacophonous and inhuman I thought I'd go mad merely from the sound.

A sound like a rising and falling shriek intertwined a wet, slopping-like splatter.

I thudded to my side, desperate to recover breath. Moving clouds over the woods unmercifully afforded more moonlight at the same instant I looked up . . .

The awkward-jointed, shuddering thing had somehow been staked to a tree via one of Onderdonk's iron stoking rods rammed into one of its orbicular eyeballs. As the impossible vocal protest wound down, it convulsed with an added sound akin to wet leather flapping.

A dark blur, then, and rapid footfalls, snagged my gaze, as I plainly saw a figure gliding away into the woods.

Who had saved me? *Mary?* I wondered, but, no, if so she'd have said something, and no woman in her stage of pregnancy could've moved so nimbly. Or perhaps a townsperson in conscientious objection to the collective's ghastly initiatives. Or . . .

Could it have been young Walter?

The madness of the previous minutes released my senses. I was still on a mission: to save Mary and her son, to see to their escape from this macabre, clandestine netherocracy. Distant thrashing in the woods told me my savior was heading west, across the road . . .

Towards Mary's house.

Recovered now, I reclaimed my pistol.

"Kill her," Zalen's head said. "Then kill yourself."

With more than a little loathe I picked the head up by its greasy hair and–

"Don't you dare, Morley!"

–dropped it into the smoker which was slow-cooking Mr. Onderdonk. Reclosing the lid, I could still hear its muffled remonstrance. "Ain't nothing but a rich pud . . ."

"But a rich pud still in possession of his head," I replied. Then I ran off–after the shape that had spared my life.

It was chiefly blind faith that guided me through the night-shrouded thicket and labyrinth of gnarled trees. Fireflies constellated the darkness. Eventually, I sighed in relief to see the squat, dark form of Mary's overgrown abode, the faintest candles glowing in the tiny windows. And–

There he is!

It was before one such window that I spied the obscure figure, the person who'd saved my life. But before I could take even a single step forward, the figure whirled, and it whisked away into the trees deft as a wood-sprite. My first impulse was to call out but then I remembered the necessity of inconspicuousness. Who knew how many other fullbloods lurked near? Nor did I run after the figure, for that would result in complete diversion to my goal. Instead, I peeked into the wanly lit pane that the figure had just quitted, and there I saw, on a pitiful sack filled with leaves and dead grass, Mary's young son Walter, asleep. It was the candle-stub and holder sitting on the crude dirt floor that gave the room its diminutive light.

I had no time for contemplations; softer and more erratic footfalls alarmed me from the southward side of the house. Pistol at the ready, I covered myself behind a tree, holding my breath . . .

The figure that stepped into a sprawl of moonlight was Mary.

She trudged forward with difficulty, obviously returning from the forced bacchanal at the lake. Wearied, then, she gasped, then buckled over and was sick. I rushed to her as she retched in misery.

"Oh, Foster!" she sobbed. "I prayed that you'd still be alive—"

"Your prayers have been answered," I said and took her up in an embrace. *But we'll need more than prayer, I'm afraid,* came an amending thought. She wore the esoteric robe of earlier, with the confounding configurations embroidered within its fringes. Her warm, heavy body trembled in my arms. "I've come for you, and your son—"

She bolted from the comfort my embrace had given her. "We must get inside, and we must keep out voices very low."

"Mary, I—"

"Shhh! You *don't* understand!" and she took my hand and pulled me into the squalor-embalmed house through a narrow, uneven door. Total dark and a dense mustiness suddenly cocooned me; it was only her warm hand I had as a guide.

She piloted me to another low-ceilinged room lit by one candle alone, make-shift furniture in evidence. I helped her sit on a milk crate-turned-chair, and when she finally caught her breath, she looked up at me with the saddest eyes. "Oh, Foster, I'm so sorry. You've jeopardized your life by coming here."

"I've come here, Mary," I asserted, "for you and your son."

Her flushed face fell into her hands. "There's so much you don't know."

"Calm yourself. I know everything now."

Astonishment forced her gaze upward. "You've-you've seen the things?"

"Yes, earlier at the lake, during the regrettable ritual that your circumstances have forced upon you, and also minutes ago, at the

Onderdonk's. One of the fullbloods nearly killed me."

"So . . . you *know* about the fullbloods?"

"I know everything. I know what's going on at the second floor of the Hilman House, I know about the dual corpse repositories in the caverns beneath the waterfront. I know why your brother Paul is infirm, and I also know that your stepfather is a crossbreed between their race and ours and that he's the only one of his kind allowed to live after the mandated genocide of years ago." I took her hand. "And, Mary, I know why they're forcing the collective's women to remain perpetually pregnant. The newborns aren't sacrificed, they're *utilized* for research intended to lead to the demise of humankind. Several hours ago I witnessed Zalen handing over several such newborns to the fullbloods, out on the sandbar."

She hitched on another sob. "Zalen? But, my God, you must think I'm a fiend for allowing my babies to be used like this."

"I think nothing of the sort," I snapped, "for I also know that you are *forced* into this perverse servitude. Should you refuse to comply, you and your family would all be slaughtered." I quieted, and gripped her hand more tightly, to assure her. "Mary, I know also of the servile tasks you were pressured to perform in the past, out of desperation, under Cyrus Zalen's pandering influence and pornographic endeavors."

She nearly gagged, tears now literally plipping from her eyes onto the dirt floor. "Then how can a moral man like you even stand to be in the same room with me?"

My verity left no margin for hesitation. "I'm in love with you, Mary. It would wound my heart forever for you to not believe this."

Her face went back to her hands. "That just makes it worse . . ."

"Why!" I demanded, perhaps too loudly. "I don't expect you to love me in return, but I can pray and live in the hope that one day you will, and should that never happen, then I will *still* love you just as much."

Now she hugged me quite suddenly, "Oh, Foster, but I *do* love you; I have since you came into the restaurant today–"

I could've collapsed in the rush ebullience that inundated my spirit. At that moment I knew that in my life of plenty I actually had nothing–until now.

Now, I had everything.

"Then why on earth do you say our love makes us *worse?*" I pleaded.

"Foster! Think about it! Lovecraft's story is *true,* and I'm living right in the middle of it."

"What Zalen didn't tell me I found out for myself."

"But, Foster–Zalen is the reason that the fullbloods are on the hunt. They're on the hunt . . . for *you.*"

"When I was at the old Innswich Point tonight, I was forced to shoot one of their reanimants, a prostitute of Zalen's," I told her, then remembered the most disturbing point. "I didn't really kill her, for she was already dead. But my shot detained her long enough to broker my escape. It's quite possible that one or more of the fullbloods saw or heard this, and even more possible that Candace informed them directly after I'd fled."

"That's not the reason, Foster," she went on, a hand to her belly as if discomfited. "It's because of Zalen, much earlier today. Sentinels are everywhere. Every single townsperson reports back to them. And some of them, like Candace, are already physically dead. One of them overheard Zalen telling you about the tunnels beneath the waterfront of Innswich Point. No one can know about that, Foster. It's one of their greatest secrets, so anyone who learns of it . . . is hunted down."

This was moot, though I should've recalled Lovecraft's story with more exploit. Even the most guarded whispers were overheard, if not by the degraded townsfolk, then by the Deep Ones themselves, whose auditory faculties were super-normal. But a paramount point collided with my deductive processes now that I'd gleaned this data. "I take it, then, we're not safe in your house. We must leave at once."

"They won't come here, Foster," she said with downcast eyes. "One of their leaders . . . has taken a fancy to me."

"You needn't be ashamed," I assured her. "Zalen mentioned this. He called them 'sovereigns'; but he also mentioned that sexual intercourse, even among these hierarchs, is banned via their new laws. I also know that the reason your brother and stepfather have been spared is due to this same sovereign's fondness for you."

She began to speak, but then bowed forward with a grimace.

"Mary! You're in pain."

"No, no, I'm all right. I just need a short rest"–she reached up. "Help me, Foster, to the bed."

I took great caution assisting her; she appeared exhausted, worn, and aching all at once. A glance to the "bed" forced a grimace on my part, for it existed as no more than the most primitive of straw mattresses. *With a little luck, she'll be sleeping in a REAL bed tomorrow, likely for the first time in her horrendously burdened life.*

A happy sigh escaped her lips. "That's much better, Foster. Thank you. Dr. Anstruther says I'll be due in another week or so."

"Anstruther," I sputtered the name with venom. "I've seen *his* handiwork. I take it he's a senior member of Olmstead's collective."

She nodded. "He's the one who runs everything here–for *them*."

"I should've known."

She lay back, sedate now, and–I pray God–banishing the profane foray at the lake from her tired mind. "Here, Foster," she murmured; she took my hand and placed it at the center of her swollen belly. "Feel the life inside."

It did so with great wonder. *A blessing,* I mused. *Each and every life is a blessing...*

"I'd like so much to keep it," came her next murmuration. Tears welled. "I'd give anything..."

"You will keep it, Mary–this I vow." The great bolus of flesh beneath the occult robe seemed to *beat* with heat. "You stay here and rest while I return to the Onderdonk's to retrieve their motor. In less than an hour's time, I'll be transporting you and Walter away from here, to the security of my estate in Providence–"

"You just don't understand," she moaned in frustration. "If I try to leave, they'll come after me. No one in the collective can *ever* leave."

"We'll see about that," I replied but still mindful of what Zalen had implied of the fates of those who had tried. "Leave it to me. I will drive you to safety or die trying."

When she looked at me, I noted something behind her eyes that could only be the desperate joy of hope.

"It just makes me love you more for wanting to do this for us. But I can't let you. We would never make it out; we'd all die."

"I'm willing to take that chance," I told her with no hesitancy whatsoever. "Are you? Would you take that chance, for Walter to finally have a good life and attend good schools like other boys? Would you take that chance"–I gave the gravid belly a momentary caress–"to give this unborn child the chance to live and to behold the beauty of the world, and to save it from the blasphemous death that awaits it otherwise?"

She sobbed, gulped, and nodded. "Yes! I *will* take the chance! Even if we all die, then at least I'll get to die with you . . ."

"Wait here," I told her, choking up. "I'll return presently," and next I was out of the house and back out into the moon-spattered night.

I did not allow myself to entertain thoughts which might divert my focus, but what a luxury that would have been. I wended back toward the Onderdonk's, eyes proverbially peeled, my Colt pistol slippery in my sweating hand. The woods were profuse with night-sounds now, where they hadn't been before. It made me wonder. If these fullblooded monstrosities were indeed on the hunt for me, I saw no hint of them all the way back to Onderdonk's ramshackle compound.

The smokers were gusting; I ignored the rich, savory–and

unmentionable–aroma. Only from the corner of my eye did I allow myself a glance at the dead creature staked to the tree. The prospect of seeing one of these abominations in detail did not incite my curiosity. Closer to the truck, I had to step around Zalen's innards and body parts, a fairly daunting task in itself, though I did spare myself one mental levity: *It couldn't have happened to a finer and more forthright gentleman.*

Good Lord! came my next distasteful thought, for when I slipped into the time-weathered vehicle, my buttocks grew immediately sopped from the deposit of Zalen's blood which had been let during his evisceration and dismemberment. I sat still a moment, to slowly survey my immediate surroundings through the windscreen, and saw nothing–absolutely *nothing*–out of the ordinary. *If these fullbloods are hunting me, they're exhibiting a less-than-fair effort thus far.* A grim reminder assailed me next, however: Zalen's earlier concern about the truck's starting mechanism. I was an antiquarian and philanthropist, not a car thief. *If it's a keyed ignition, then I'll have no choice but to drag Onderdonk's half-cooked corpse from the smoker and search his pockets for the key . . .* I withdrew my pocket-flash, closed my shooting eye to preserve its night-vision, then, for just a split-second, turned on the flash before the dashboard.

My heart fell like a stone.

What my flash illumined was a cylindrical keyway mounted in the dash.

"Here's the key, Mr. Morley," the small but sudden voice whispered just outside the open truck window. Where my heart had just sunk in the worst despair it nearly jettisoned from my mouth in the coming shock.

It was young Walter who stood beside the vehicle.

"In Heaven's name, son!" I snapped a whisper back to him. "You nearly stopped my heart!" but then my eyes flicked to his adolescent hand and proved what he claimed was true. "How . . . How on earth did you–"

A modest smile of pride touched his face. "Mr. Onderdonk would always keep the key beneath his door mat; I've seen him put it there a lot, sir, during my hikes through the woods."

"Not only a lad of proper manners," I gushed, "but one of industriousness." I blinked. "But you were asleep only a short time ago."

"I woke up and heard you and my mom talking, so I came out on my own, to get the key for you."

This was certainly a gift I could never have anticipated. "You're a fine boy, Walter, and a very brave one. But it's unduly dangerous out here. Do you know about . . . ," but then the sentence deteriorated.

"I know all about the fullbloods, sir. I've seen them a few times, but tonight, I've seen a whole lot of them."

And it's my fault, I reminded myself. Walter's courage was commendable but it did indeed put him in great danger. "Get in next to me, Walter. We're going to pick up your mother so I can take you both to live with me."

"But you'll need help, sir," he added. "It would be best if I position myself in the back of the truck. I can't get a good aim if I'm inside with you."

"A good *aim?* Walter, whatever are you talking about?"

He raised his handmade bow. "They may try to block the road back to the house, but I'm a pretty good shot."

I smiled in spite of myself. "Lad, you're surely the bravest boy to ever walk these parts but I'm afraid that suction-cup arrows will do little good against the fullbloods."

Then he showed me a handful of *real* arrows.

"See, Mr. Morley? We better go, before they come."

What could I say to such youthful ingenuity and unhesitant bravado? "All right, Walter. Get in back and be vigilant . . . And keep your fingers crossed that this old vehicle starts."

The boy hopped in back. With wide eyes, then, and a trembling lip, I inserted the key into the cylinder, uttered a prayer that seemed dismally anemic, and turned the key.

The rusted hulk hitched, gave off a loud metallic whine that made the tendons in my neck stand out, then rumbled to a start. I ground gears in my attempt to get it in first, gritted my teeth at a long grind, then we were finally moving. The vehicle was indeed roadworthy, but in that evidence, the noise its starting had made could surely be heard from here to town.

I pulled out and turned posthaste, gravel and oyster shells popping beneath worn tires. "Keep a sharp eye!" I called to Walter when I considered the necessity to leave the headlamps off. "Yes, Mr. Morley!" he replied, and when I glanced back through the hole which had once housed glass, I saw the lad positioned in back, his crude bow at the ready. I knew that at an identical age, I'd have been in possession of not one-tenth of the boy's courage. *I'll raise him as though he were my own,* I vowed, *and be the father he'd never had, and the same for Mary's baby . . .* Rusted springs ground when I throttled the archaic vehicle across the rutted road to town. The moon seemed to spray its light upon us for the few seconds that the road exposed us, such that the road itself and the trees and vegetation lining it seemed iridescent, and this made me think of Lovecraft's masterpiece, "The Color Out of Space," said to be his personal favorite. Though my fear levels jumped from this brief exposure, it enabled me to view the road both ways. Where I expected to glimpse enemies, I saw, again, virtually nothing in the way of detractors.

Strange, I thought. *Unless they're lying in wait . . .*

The enfeebled truck rocked when I traversed the wheel and navigated into the long, heavily wooded dirt-scratch lane which would lead us to the house. Suddenly darkness swallowed us, only minutely dappled by the moon, for the boughs of overhead trees nearly connected with one another from either side, transposing our route into that of a tunnel. I had to retard speed considerably now, for the reduced visibility.

Walter's wan face peered in to the rear hole. "Mr. Morley?

Maybe you should turn on the headlamps. I can't see a *thing!*"

The light-discipline of a soldier surely had tactical exceptions, not to mention that I was nothing remotely similar to a soldier. *Just a rich pud,* I recalled Zalen's slight, but he was right. I fancied I could hear him laughing at me now, even as his odious head continued to cook. But now I would *have* to be a soldier, and I would have to take chances in order to achieve success. I took the lad's advice, and switched on the headlamps.

The boy shrieked, and so did I.

Figures rushed forward out of the bramble-carpeted woods. Before I could even make transitive reaction, I saw a queerly robed figure–but one with a clearly human face–lunge forward but then buckle back, his hand shooting to his face as an arrow caught him right in his opened mouth.

"Good shot, Walter!"

When a hand–a human hand, not the webbed extremity I expected–shot into the passenger window, I thrust my pistol-filled fist toward it, then–

BAM!

The lucky shot caught the marauder right in the adam's apple. Bubbly blood shot from the wound as the robed predator screamed.

And it was a man I recognized. *Mr. Wraxall, the restaurant owner . . .*

These were not the monstrous fullbloods I anticipated to be set for ambush, but townsmen, all dressed in those same robes with esoteric fringe. More snatches of faces were revealed: the hotel clerk, the maintenance man, the diner who'd been lunching with his paramour at the restaurant, and others. When two more shot out from left and right, Walter struck one in the shoulder; the aggressor unwisely hesitated where he stood, then was bellowing as the vehicle's wheels drubbed him beneath the chassis. The second assailant tried to climb into my open window where I easily fired a shot directly into the top of his head. He fell away, but not before I could recognize the face in the hood's oval: Dr. Anstruther.

Sin or not, I chuckled at the cad's death, and considered the splotches of his grey matter upon my shirt a unique badge of honor.

The rest of the road to the house was clear.

Where I'd expected the opposition to be formidable, I found only sheepshank weakness in its place. The squat house now came into view at the end of the headlamps' beams.

"This was almost too easy, Walter," I called out behind me. "And that troubles me quite a bit." I killed the motor, hopped out. "We must hurry now and fetch your mother. Between the engine-noise and my pistol, there'll be more after us . . ."

I sprang to the vehicle's rear bed to lift Walter out, but—

Oh, my God in Heaven, no . . .

The only objects occupying this space were the boy's meager bow and the final can of petrol.

I glanced out into the woods but saw and heard nothing.

How could I have let this happen? I condemned myself. *The town collective snatched Walter out of the back . . . and have taken him away . . .*

4

A half-hour's desperate search in the woods yielded no positive result, and to search longer would only jeopardize the possibility of getting Mary and her unborn out alive. Hence, I trudged back to the brick-and-ivy-netted hovel like a man on his way to the gallows. What could I tell Mary? Her son had been abducted and most likely was dead already–all under my charge . . .

The very normal sound of crickets followed me back inside, but then came another sound, one which actually deflected my all-pervading muse of despair:

The sound of a baby crying.

I plunged out of the foyer's ink-like murk into the candle-lit room, where the sound of infantile crying hijacked my gaze toward the heap of a mattress. "Mary!"

There she sat, bearing an exhausted smile as she sat upright among makeshift pillows. In her arms, pressed to her swelling bosom, was a newly born babe, swaddled in linens.

"I went into labor just after you left," she said, rosy-cheeked. "And then it happened only minutes later." She turned the infant for me to see.

A miracle, I thought. It was as perfect as any babe I'd ever beheld. The moment it took notice of me, it quieted, and looked at me wide-eyed.

"See, he likes you, Foster. Just the sight of you calms him." Mary rocked him as best she could.

"What a wonder," I whispered. "I'm only sorry I wasn't here to assist when the time came."

"Each time it's easier," she informed. "There was barely any pain with this one." She glanced hopefully to me, eyes aglint in the candlelight. "But we must name him right away, in case–"

In case we die trying to leave, I finished for her.

"I'm going to name him Foster," she said.

I went speechless, a tear beading in my eye.

Then her hopeful glance turned hard as granite. "And they're *not* going to get this one. Only over my dead body . . ."

The joy of this notice crested in my heart, but then crashed to the most stygian depths.

She still didn't know that Walter was gone.

"Mary, I . . . I . . ."

"I love you so much, Foster," she interrupted, teary-eyed herself. "I want you to marry me. I want to spend the rest of my life with you, and raise this child with you . . . and make love to you every single night . . ."

The words, greater than any gift I'd ever been given, only dragged my spirit deeper into the abyss of black verity.

"You, me, and Walter," she mused on, breast-feeding now. "We'll be such a happy family."

Sorrow sealed my throat like a strangler's gasp. I could barely hack out, "Mary, you don't understand. It's about—"

"I know what it's about," her placid voice came to me. "It's about Walter."

I stared.

"I never got the chance to explain earlier," she went on, modestly covering enough of her bosom to forestall my view. "Earlier, you said that you'd witnessed Cyrus Zalen at the waterfront, delivering sacks of newborns to the fullbloods."

"But-but . . . but Mary, what—"

"Don't *worry*, sweetheart. You were simply mistaken."

"Mistaken?" I asked but by now my mind was thoroughly disarranged. "No, no, Mary, I saw him, it was Zalen."

"You saw a man in a black raincoat is what you saw, Foster. Right?"

"Why . . . yes."

She looked right at me. "Foster, the man stalking you in the woods earlier today wasn't Zalen."

The comment took me aback. "But . . . I thought sure."

"And the man you saw out on the sandbar tonight wasn't Zalen, either."

"Who, then?" I demanded.

Mary squirmed in her seat, candlelight pale on her face. "It was Walter's father–"

"What!"

"Foster . . . turn around."

The cryptic command reversed my position, and my eyes blossomed at the surreal sight.

It was a man tall and gaunt who stood in the opposite corner. The black raincoat seemed several sizes too large, and its hood draped most of his face. More important was the minor burden in his arms: it was Walter. At first I feared the boy was dead but then I noted the rise and fall of his young chest.

"This is Walter's father," Mary told me in the struggling light. "Those times you mistook him as Zalen stalking you, he was actually coming here, to catch a glimpse of his son."

I suppose I already knew via some blackly ethereal portent, even before the figure retracted the hood to reveal the face of Howard Phillips Lovecraft.

I stood, lax-jawed, dizzy–staring at the icon as if beholding a vision from the highest precipice of the earth . . .

The voice which issued from the thin lips sounded high but parched, an exerted whisper. He hefted the living weight. "My son is in no danger, sir; he's merely fainted from the shock of his abduction by several of the town's collective members. Please rest assured that these self-same abductors are no longer among the living."

"You killed them?"

The thin face nodded. "Just as I killed the fullblood that was after you at the Onderdonk's. And as Mary has informed you, *I* was the ferryman you glimpsed on the sandbar tonight." The voice teetered now between cracking and high-pitchedness, hollow yet somehow exhibiting depth at the same time. "In the amalgam of my damnable

151

onus. This nefarious deed has been my province alone, since the sixteenth of March, nineteen hundred and thirty-seven."

The day after his death, I knew. The Master's words sounded ruined, like thin-membraned things blown through fence-slats in the wind. The obscene circumvention of death left his narrow visage pallored as if old mortician's wax had been applied to a skull. This semi-translucence caused me to shudder, as did his eye-whites which more resembled dirt-flecked snowcrust.

"And as you've already been partially apprized," he grated on, "the detestable creatures which I fictionalized as 'the Deep Ones' are in possession of aggressive philtres which re-synthesize nucleotide activity within a certain helical infrastructure that exists in every human cell. This ingenious–and diabolic–process has the power to, among other things, reconstitute life in the dead. Hence, sir, my damnation and the recompense for my sins."

"Your . . . *sins?*" I questioned. "But you've been known throughout your natural life as an atheist. The concept of sin is one you don't believe in."

"Not *my* conception," the haunted man intoned, "but *their* conception."

"Whatever do you mean?"

"I penned *The Shadow Over Innsmouth* close to a decade ago, but, lo, in its flaw, it was never published, and in its not being published, word never traced back to the fullbloods of its existence . . ."

"But that all changed," I hazarded, "in late-1936, when the Visionary Publications copy became available to the public. And word got back–"

"–back to the eternal monstrosities who hold sway over this place, yes. But they didn't endeavor to pursue me then–it was already known that I was suffering from a terminal affliction. Several months later, however, when I died, word of my decease riposted back to them as well. The night after I was buried, a troop of the accurst things came up out of Narragansett Bay, exhumed me, and re-enlivened my pitiable corpse. Since then I've been forced to serve them, in a number of abominable fashions whose details I'll spare you. The nexus of my punishment, though, and I should think it quite perceptible now, is the delivery of all newborns to the fullbloods' soul-dead machinations."

My throat suddenly shriveled. "They brought you back for that. To be a servitor for them."

"That and far, far worse, sir. But an unwilling traitor to my race, and the devil's package boy. The only way to protect the life of my son was to perform as I'm commanded, and deliver the innocent newborns into *their* appalling clutches." The dead eyes looked to Mary and her now-sleeping baby. "It is a task I shall never discharge again." He placed Walter down alongside Mary, then returned his attention to me. "And of you, sir, I must beg a favor."

"But I owe you my life," I exclaimed. "The beast at Onderdonk's was only moments away from killing me before you intervened–"

"Do as you have promised," the ghost-voice quavered, "and deliver Mary and my son to safety."

"I will. This I pledge–"

But in my own hesitation, I recalled something crucial while on the same hand Mary's attitude seemed suddenly crestfallen.

"Your brother, Mary. And your stepfather," I commenced with the dark implication.

"I know," she acknowledged. "Paul's not here. He sleeps in the backroom at the store."

The looks we all shared told all.

"We'll have no choice but to leave him. A rescue attempt would grossly reduce our chances of safe escape with Walter and the baby . . ."

"I'll see to the task of relieving him of his misery myself," Lovecraft offered. "The fullbloods will kill him once they learn that Mary has fled the collective, and they'll do so in a manner most grueling and torturous. I'll be certain to get to him before they have occasion to. He'll suffer not an iota of pain."

"My stepfather, though," Mary half-sobbed. "He's in the next room, and I'm afraid . . ."

She needn't finish. He would have to be euthanized, and since I was the one with the gun– "This room here?" I asked of the crude and slightly tilted wooden door to the side.

She gulped and nodded.

"All right then." I withdrew my handgun, edged toward the door.

Mary struggled to her feet to come near me. "But, Foster, you must understand. My stepfather–he's almost completely gone over by now."

"Gone over?"

Lovecraft picked up the explanation, "The metamorphosis which afflicts the crossbreeds not only taints their physical features but, I regret to impart, also their *mental* faculties. It's a certain eventuality that such hybrids in advanced age such as Mary's stepfather become hostile with time and adopt aspects of the mentality, attitudes, and sentiments of the fullbloods."

"It's true, Foster," Mary added. "He's worse now than ever. If you go in there, he'll attack you."

Then so be it, I thought, but as I approached the door Lovecraft stopped me with a hand to my shoulder. "You are not expendable, sir, but I am. It's a much more difficult event to kill a dead man than one who's still living."

"But I feel it's my responsibility," I uttered.

"You mustn't take the chance," he insisted. "You're Mary and Walter's only hope. Save your ammunition." He took the gun and returned it to my pocket, then from his own extracted a razor-sharp fileting knife. "When I'm not detained for other, more monstrous duties, the fullbloods force me to filet fish in the workhouses, and it just so happens"–he shuddered at the thought–"I *hate* fish." His ruined eyes addressed me more directly. "Go now. Take them out of here now . . . and fulfill your pledge to me."

"But-but," I stammered, still not quite reckoning the fact that it was Lovecraft in my actual midst, maloccluded jaw and all. "You could come with us."

"No, it's time for nature to take its true course," his voice wisped. "My existence has perverted death for too long. Tonight--I'll see to it--I shall be dead for good," and then he picked up the still-unconscious Walter, placed him in my arms, then assisted Mary and the baby toward the door.

Mary tried all she could to stifle her sobs as we stepped back out into the teeming night. Lovecraft bid nothing more as an adieu; he merely cast a final glance at the boy in my arms, then quietly closed the door.

I stowed my passengers all in the front of the vehicle but was stalled by a sudden and very grotesque coercion. "Foster!" shot Mary's diminutive whisper. "Where are you going?"

"Just . . . one moment," I told her, and then it was this coercion that prompted me back to the hovel of a house.

To the back window . . .

I *had* to look in, for earlier in the afternoon I'd only glimpsed the fringes of Mary's stepfather as it sat back in shadow. My eyes, now, held wide on the drab glass pane when the room's utter darkness was broken by the inner door opening, and Lovecraft undiscouragedly entered the room, candlestick in hand. That is when I saw Mary's stepfather in detail . . .

The thing lay sidled over on the floor, breathing with a sound like bubbles being blown under water. When it noticed Lovecraft's presence, a head that looked squashed down flinched. Mary had said that her stepfather had now fully "gone over," but I could see that the metamorphosis was not yet totally complete. One eye was indeed froglike in that it existed half out of its socket, with a glistening green-black lid. A gold iris glittered amid the great, peach-sized orb; however its other eye appeared far more human, and the amalgamation of these opposites only heightened the grotesquerie of this living result of breeding between two separate species. Two mere holes functioned as the nose; fissures that could only be gills pulsed at its throat, and overall the skin seemed a queer combination of toad and man.

Then the wide rim of the creature's mouth snapped open and–

sssssssssssnap!

–out shot a sickly pink cord which could only suffice for its tongue. Immediately I recalled the details of my glimpse through this window earlier in the day, where the same deformed and disjointed figure that Walter referred to as his "gramps" vollied the same cord that I'd then mistaken for a whip. But now I saw that it was no whip; it was a narrow yet heavily veined tentacle, rife with minute suckers which pulsed beneath a repugnant glisten. The appalling, boneless appendage was deftly forestalled by Lovecraft's wrist, whereupon he sliced the tentacle off with his knife.

Its pain was readily apparent as arms only vaguely human sprang up in protest. The lopsided head shuddered, the great rimmed mouth locked open in order to release a vociferation that could only have been born in hell: a whistle like a tea kettle interlaced by the slopping, wet spattery scream I'd heard a facsimile of earlier. When it tried to rise on joints that flexed backwards, Lovecraft came more definitely forward with his fileting knife . . .

I trotted away, unable to bear any more of this dismal execution. When the tenor and volume of the crossbreed's scream quadrupled, I knew the grim task had been done.

With a blank mind, then, I started the rickety vehicle and pulled off. Smoke gusted and springs creaked, but now the truck was barreling down the road away from the awful house that Mary would never again have to enter.

The road south seemed the most direct shot, and its first quarter mile stood miraculously clear. Around a bend, though–

Mary and I screamed in unison.

It was a veritable barricade of monsters which occluded the pass.

156

Fifty of them? A hundred? The logistics scarcely mattered. The sweep of our headlights compounded the sight to an utter vision of chaos: green-glistening skin pocked by brown, toadlike bumps, eyes jutting from compressed, earless heads like balls of black glass. Though they all stood upright, they showed white, runneled underbellies and legs corded with strange muscles. Dangling, horrific genitals told me they were predominantly male. Their height fluctuated between five to seven feet, though even in their upright stances, most were half-hunched over, so God knew their *true* height. Dare I barrel forward in an attempt to mow them down? Were I alone I may have risked this, but with Mary and her children in my charge, I knew I couldn't.

The sight froze, maximizing the horror of what we beheld. The mass of abominations stood there, flexed on corded muscles, and as the headlamps blared, they all leaned back, tilted their heads upward, and then, as if on psychic command, their hideous rimmed mouths all opened at once and they began to shriek.

The sound caused the very woods to vibrate: a phlegmatic keening blended with the sound of a thousand men marching quickly through muck. If sound could cause physical impact, this was surely the case for the cacophony, now, made the truck visibly rock. I'm sure I was screaming myself as I threw the decrepit vehicle into reverse, but even at the top of my lungs my own utterance of fear could not be heard over the unearthly mudslide of sound which was being vaulted at us. Mary had already passed out so she did not have to see what I glimpsed in that last half-second before I could turn fully around . . .

With the fullbloods' screams of objection, the tongue of each and every one of them jettisoned from their mouths. Unlike Mary's stepfather, whose hybrid tongue was but a single pink tentacle, each of these monsters possessed a tongue comprised of at least a dozen of the same, glistening and sucker-pocked appendages. Each clump of deranged tongues seemed to twist into a single, fat pulsing column and shivered there in mid-air throughout the entirety of their vocal display. These columns of detestable flesh *had* to extend at least five feet.

157

I fully depressed the accelerator pedal when I'd managed to turn around to a northward heading. Did my eyes deceive me when I dared to take one glance in the rearward mirror? I could've sworn they were pursuing me now–the entire mass of the things–and some seemed to be leaping forward at bounds of twenty feet, which barely afforded the speeding vehicle any distance ahead of them. It took me a half mile, in fact, to gain any comfortable ground, but just as I'd realized this–

I screamed again and slammed on the truck's brakes.

At least twice as many fullbloods blocked the northward way out. *My God, what can I do now?* When I looked over my shoulder through the truck's former rear window, I could see the first of the southern detachment coming round the bend, bringing their vocal storm with them, but I noticed something else as well . . .

The can of gasoline that had been in back previously was no longer there.

Where it had gone to, I hardly had time to consider. Now, it seemed, I had no choice but to try to plow through this mass to the north. The baby was wailing now, and Walter finally roused, too, only to glimpse the horrific sight before us.

"Say your prayers, Walter," I urged, and then the fullbloods ahead of us began to shamble forward. In less then a minute, I knew, we'd be converged upon from north and south.

As I would utter my own last prayer and plunged the accelerator in a feeble attempt to plow through the monstrous blockade, young Walter pointed left and cried out, "Mr. Morley! Who's that man there?"

Man? my shattered faculties managed, but when I looked I saw the black-raincoated form of Lovecraft waving assertively at us. He was urging me to veer the truck left, into a narrow trail that looked barely able admit the vehicle's width.

I saw, too, that it was *he* who'd taken the fuel can from the truck's rear bed. The can hung from his hand.

When I pulled into the trail, I saw the northward mass of beasts shift into the woods themselves, as if to try to cut me off before I could drive to wherever the road would take us. Shortly thereafter the southern mass poured into the trail behind us. The sound they made caused the forest to tremor: the wet, slopping gush detailed by wave after wave of inhuman caterwauls. At this point, the forest was verminous with the shambling, bump-skinned things.

Then the woods began to shift with crackling light . . .

"A fire!" Walter shouted.

I could see it all too easily now as I pressed the feeble truck to the extent of its mechanical possibilities. A virtual *wall* of flame spread through the woods just behind the encroaching ranks, and when I looked desperately south, I saw another wall spreading. Lovecraft had obviously walked a line of petrol on either side of the trail, igniting them only when the dual masses of ichthyic creatures had proceeded deeply enough to be trapped. This month of steadfast drought had turned the forest floor and brambles to a tinder-dry state, and now it was all combusting almost simultaneously. Orange, wavering light pressed us in now, and the sound of crackling woods soon overcame the volume of the fullbloods' wretched howls, their unearthly battle-cry quickly transposing to sounds of utter consternation. In only a minute or two our entire surroundings were aflame.

Our adversaries were trapped in the woods now by two encroaching walls of fire. The things were trapped, yes.

But so were we.

Each fire-line seemed to follow the truck's progress. The most stifling heat surged inward, and when glancing to either side I saw mad, inhuman figures thrashing, flopping, convulsing in the ignited woods, dressed in suits of fire. The rearview showed me the narrow trail completely engulfed, with ghost-shapes of blistering *things* as they were incinerated alive. Just as the fire began to engulf the truck . . .

I could've swooned at the sight.

The trail disgorged us into a moon-lit clearing.

"We're out!" Walter shouted.

"We made it," came my own disbelieving whisper. I maintained my headway, though, for fear that some of the fullbloods must have escaped the conflagration, but when at a safe distance, I idled to a halt and looked back on the fiery scene . . .

Walter's gaze joined my own. Now the fires were spreading outward, smoke pouring off treetops and billowing in the sky. The macabre, bellicose howls of hundreds of fullbloods now wound down to pathetic and periodic squeals. It was the crackling of massive flames that drowned out all else.

"What . . . What happened?" Mary asked, bewildered, the baby asleep at her bosom. "It looks like the entire woods are on fire."

"They will be if we don't get away from here now," I realized, and back into gear the truck went, and we were off. Walter's fortunate knowledge of the area, due to his nature walks, took us to another narrow trail which emptied us out onto the main road into town in only minutes. All that followed us now was the most eerie silence.

"Mr. Morley?" Walter inquired. "That man in the raincoat saved us."

"Indeed, he did, Walter."

"I know I've seen him in the woods before, many times, but I never got very close to him. Who *was* that man?"

I took Mary's hand. "One day, Walter, your mother and I will tell you . . ."

Not too long after that, a sign gave relieving notice that we were about to exit onto State Route Number One. With a smidgen of luck, we'd be in Providence by dawn.

5

The passing of six months has brought me many joyous changes. The sale of my Providence mansion–to a Standard Oil executive, no less–has left me even wealthier than before. A dead man's words–Zalen's–never left my cognizance: *They travel along any existing waterway, and they're very fast.* Now that God had granted my new standing as a family man, I relocated only days after that night of incogitable horror, to a place where there existed *no* waterways for fifty miles in any direction, in the 36th state of the union, Nevada. My fortune built us an impregnable adobe house situated in the middle of the region's most arid land, just south of the state's dead-center point. Alkaline mud-plains, sand-swept desert, and endless square miles of sagebrush and tumbleweed provide the vista anywhere one might happen to peer.

And–to reiterate–there are no waterways.

I bank in Carson City over a hundred miles northwest, and from there fresh water for drinking and bathing is trucked in weekly. Also trucked in weekly are shifts of Pinkerton guards, who live at the house and keep watch round the clock. They believe I'm merely a successful businessman leery of enemies of the trade. Naturally I've never told them exactly what it is I fear may one day encroach the house in the middle of the night.

As for Olmstead and its waterfront sector formerly known as Innswich Point, I can only recount what I'd gleaned from the newspapers: the great drought-stoked forest fire had scorched thousands of surrounding acres. Of the 361 registered residents, none were known to have survived, many having been incinerated in ill-fated evacuation attempts, and the rest having died from smoke-inhalation as the fires, as devastating as they'd been, had not actually burned the town's new block-and-concrete architecture. How had the fires commenced? Lightning, the sources said. But the region could sigh in relief, since a rainstorm the very next day had prevented the conflagration from spreading to even more devastating ambits.

Curiously, a final paragraph mentioned federal inspectors examining the town's remains days later, but no explanation was rendered for such inspections. Nor was any quantity of information offered for the government's demolitioning of certain sectors of the town's waterfront. For safety reasons, was all they said. And no mention, of course, was made of any dead person found to be wearing a scrimy black raincoat . . .

Mary and I were wed very shortly after relocating, and the life I've always dreamed of is now at hand. Live-in tutors educate young Walter, and I couldn't be more delighted to relate that he's taken on a similar academic and creative bent to his father. A nanny, too, was hired on, to assist Mary with the rearing of the infant that she'd so complimentarily named Foster. Whichever Sire consigned to that accursed and evil-saturated second floor of the Hilman House had actually fathered the child, it mattered not. *I* was now the infant's father, and it was a station in life I felt blessed to have.

Hence . . .

Happily ever after, as the old cliche goes. Except, perhaps, for the nights, where I sleep less than soundly with my Colt Hammerless beneath my pillow and find myself rising at odd hours to scan the all-encompassing scrubland with my field glasses and to check on the night-guards to satisfy myself than no unmentionable marauders had surprised them under the cover of darkness . . .

Mary is pregnant again, in her sixth month, the doctor estimates. My celibacy had ended quite passionately on our wedding night, and her zeal for my body as well as my love only gives me cause to thank God all the more for such a blessing. But this, dear reader, subsumes my only potential calamity.

You'll likely be asking yourself what could possibly be deemed *calamitous* about wedlock in the eyes of God and the sequent wonder of the miraculous union which brings forth new life.

At the very least, I'm reckoning it quite well, I believe. You see, it wasn't until after our marriage that Mary, with quite a bit of trepidation, admitted that only minutes after having given birth to Foster–and whilst Walter and I were out fetching Onderdonk's truck– her genetically deranged stepfather had raped her quite fastidiously. But whether it was my own seed that impregnated her or the tainted seed of that crossbred thing . . .

Only time will tell.

ABOUT THE AUTHOR

Edward Lee has authored close to 50 books in the field of horror; he specializes in hardcore fare. His most recent novels are LUCIFER'S LOTTERY and the Lovecraftian THE HAUNTER OF THE THRESHOLD. His movie HEADER was released on DVD by Synapse Film in June, 2009. Lee lives in Largo, Florida.

"Squid Pulp Blues" Jordan Krall - In these three bizarro-noir novellas, the reader is thrown into a world of murderers, drugs made from squid parts, deformed gun-toting veterans, and a mischievous apocalyptic donkey.

". . . with SQUID PULP BLUES, [Krall] created a wholly unique terrascape of Ibsen-like naturalism and morbidity; an extravaganza of white-trash urban/noir horror."
- Edward Lee

"Apeshit" Carlton Mellick III - Friday the 13th meets Visitor Q. Six hipster teens go to a cabin in the woods inhabited by a deformed killer. An incredibly fucked-up parody of B-horror movies with a bizarro slant

"The new gold standard in unstoppable fetus-fucking kill-freakomania . . . Genuine all-meat hardcore horror meets unadulterated Bizarro brainwarp strangeness. The results are beyond jaw-dropping, and fill me with pure, un-forgivable joy." - John Skipp

"Super Fetus" Adam Pepper - Try to abort this fetus and he'll kick your ass!

"The story of a self-aware fetus whose morally bankrupt mother is desperately trying to abort him. This darkly humorous novella will surely appall and upset a sizable percentage of people who read it... In-your-face, allegorical social commentary."
- BarnesandNoble.com

"Fistful of Feet" Jordan Krall -   A bizarro tribute to Spaghetti westerns, Featuring Cthulhu-worshipping Indians, a woman with four feet, a Giallo-esque serial killer, a crazed gunman who is obsessed with sucking on candy, Syphilis-ridden mutants, ass juice, burping pistols, sexually transmitted tattoos, and a house devoted to the freakiest fetishes.

"Krall has quite a flair for outrage as an art form."
- Edward Lee

AVAILABLE FROM AMAZON.COM

Lightning Source UK Ltd.
Milton Keynes UK
UKOW031128080512

192172UK00006B/103/P

9 781936 383115